The *Tora* *Island* *Adventure*

Alyy Lavinia O'Leary

The Tora Island Adventure
by
Alyy Lavinia O'Leary

This paperback edition First Published in Great Britain
in 2022 by Beercott Books.

Text © Alyy Lavinia O'Leary 2021

Cover design & map illustration © Simon Lucas 2022

Design & layout © Beercott Books 2022

ISBN 978-1-9163953-6-7

A catalogue record of this book is available
from the British Library.

Beercott Books
www.beercottbooks.co.uk

CONTENTS

Tora North

Tora Northeast

Arena City

Tora South

Tora
Island

CHAPTER ONE
Cause and Effect

There are only a few things in life we can be absolutely sure of, the rest, as they say, is a throw of the dice. We know the sun comes up and goes down, the moon and the stars come out every night, and the sea lends us its tide, for a short time, before greedily snatching it back. The most underestimated certainty is cause and effect, that every action provokes a reaction, be it mild or monstrous, and one is assured, its' consequence is waiting to reveal itself.

And so, a series of events began to unfold which led to the beautiful fall evening when Bubo, the magic owl, decided to enter a parallel universe at 200 Scott Drive, Connecticut, U.S.A, the Earth. As he transitioned from one universe to the other, there was an intense flash of light, for just a split second, and then his speedy entrance slowed to a comfortable glide. As Bubo relaxed, he forgot the precious item he held in his mouth, and it fell, twirling its way down, into the colourful, New England undergrowth. Bubo searched and searched, but, even with his exceptional eyesight, he could not see the package camouflaged amongst the autumn leaves. He decided, after a long search, to return to his home on Tora Island before Queen Draxa missed him. It wouldn't be long before she realised that something very important had gone missing from her chamber and he needed to be by her side, to divert any suspicion of his part in its disappearance. He would have to come back to this universe later and hoped, against hope, the package would be safe in its woody wrapping. The fate of the kingdom depended on it, and with that hope, he aimed for the portal and evaporated from sight with a lightning strike.

That very same lightning strike distracted Mrs. Applegate, a seventy-eight-year-old widow who was taking her evening walk in the woods.

The giant trees: Maples, Birch, Pine, Aspen and Cedar, to name but a few, bordered her back yard on Scott Drive and since her husband's passing, she found comfort in their ever-changing beauty and even talked to them, as though they were her family. Bubo's exit lit up the sky above her and for a moment she looked statuesque, with her face tilted upward and her right leg in mid-air, ready to trample on Queen Draxa's possession. She managed to steady herself just in the nick of time.

"Oh children! What have we got here?"

She slowly bent over and picked up a majestic looking scroll wrapped in a gold ribbon.

"Heavens to Besty! What a fine-looking thing! I wonder what's inside?"

She carefully untied it and could see in the dim evening light a drawing or perhaps, even a painting of a young man. From his build, she guessed he was around her eldest grandson's age, maybe fifteen or so. He was dressed in rather grand clothing, reminiscent of Ancient Greece. The funny thing was he didn't have a face.

What's the use of an unfinished portrait, children?" She said, tutting to herself and slowly made her way home.

The scroll lay abandoned on Mrs. Applegate's kitchen countertop for a couple of days before her daughter, Laura, and her youngest grandson, Jake, a popular seventh grader, voted most caring in the class yearbook, turned up to collect a donation for the school fundraiser.

"Mom, it's me and Jakie. Have you got the charity box organised?"

"Yes honey," Mrs. Applegate said as she came through the kitchen door, coaxing the last slurp of her berry smoothie from the cup.

"Mmmm....delicious! Hey Jakie! How are ya? Gosh! You grow bigger every time I see you! How old are you now?"

"Twelve, Grandma. Same as the last time you asked me."

His mother shot him one of those looks where her eyebrows arched like a caterpillar, a sure sign of an impending grounding if he didn't behave himself.

"Mom, the box?" queried Laura to the old woman.

"Yes honey, on the counter over there," said Mrs. Applegate pointing to an area strewn with newspapers, magazines, junk mail, a couple of rolls of wrapping paper, a new box of Christmas cards and ... The scroll.

"Honestly Mother, I'm surprised you can find anything amongst all this mess?"

"It's not a mess darling, rather organised chaos," she said as she handed over her unwanted items for the sale.

"Grandma, what's this?" Jake was waving the scroll in the air.

Oh, somethin' and nothin', Mrs. Applegate replied, "I found it in the woods. It's just a half-finished portrait. Why don't you take it? Someone might like to finish it?"

"Thanks Grannie, I will. We need to raise as much money as we can to help our twin school in Africa. We are going to buy them some new computers!"

And with that, Jake and his mother carried the things to the car and drove the few miles to the middle school and set up their stall. Lots of his school friends had stalls too. His friend and next-door neighbour, Maddie, was selling cupcakes. Partners in crime since kindergarten, her dramatic personality always added a little spice to any proceedings. She waved at him and started to make her way over.

"I brought you a couple over before they go. I know chocolate is your favourite!"

"Gee, thanks Maddie!" Jake swiped the cupcakes from the plate and stuffed them into his mouth as though his life depended on it.

"Jacob!" His mother reproached him.

There goes that caterpillar again! He thought to himself.

In the few minutes it took for Jake's stuffed cheeks to deflate, Maddie had a cursory glance over his wares and instantly picked up the scroll.

"Oooh! This looks interesting. What is it?" She said, a big mischievous smile beamed across her face as she proceeded to untie the ribbon.

"Oh Wow! I love it! I could finish it for my art project at school."

"And a bargain at just five dollars!" Said Jake, trying to sound like a real salesman.

"Gee thanks Jake! You wanna come over to my house tonight? We could play some video games."

"Okay. See ya later."

That evening, after a very lucrative car boot sale, Jake made his way over to Maddie's house. Their houses were adjacent to one another, with only a small stretch of lawn between them and they could easily talk from their bedroom windows. When he arrived home all he wanted to do was flop on his bed and chill out, however, he could see Maddie gesticulating wildly for him to come over. Standing at her front door he wondered what all the fuss was about.

"What?" He asked, his hands open in front of him, reiterating the question.

"You are soooooo not going to believe this!"

Maddie's sense of the dramatic heightened the intrigue. She grabbed his armed and dragged him up the stairs and into her room.

"Look at this! Look at this!" She exclaimed.

The scroll was laid out flat on her desk, with small paper weights at each corner.

"Yea, it's the unfinished portrait." So what? Jake said, none the wiser.

"Watch. Just watch," instructed Maddie, her eyes wide, mouth half smiling.

She picked up a pencil and presented it in front of Jake with a dramatic flourish and then began to draw in eyes, nose, and mouth.

"Like I said Mad, so what?" Jake was really tired and starting to feel more than a tad frustrated. Still, Maddie pointed at the picture, her finger outstretched and rigid with excitement. To his amazement, the features began to disappear.

"It's the same with every pen, pencil or paint I try, explained Maddie, the face just won't stay!"

"That is so freaky!"

"What do you think it means Jake?"

"I don't know. The paper looks kinda old though."

"Maybe I should it take to art class tomorrow. Mr. Peterson might be able to help?"

"Great idea," said Jake.

As mesmerised as he was by this new mystery, he could not ignore his grumbling tummy, stirred by the waft of the fall barbecue coming from his backyard and into Maddie's bedroom.

"Gotta go Mads," he said, licking his lips, "see you after school!"

CHAPTER TWO

Queen Draxa

The climate on Tora Island, North was generally temperate and today was no exception. It was the kind of day that made its people stop what they were doing, be it milking a cow, trading their wares in the market, or fishing off the undulating waters of the island's coastline, and just...... breathe. The still and calm of that moment was cut short by the shrill, echoing, maniacal scream of Queen Draxa, as it pierced its way to the outer most regions of the land. Since the death of her husband, King Leonex, the kingdom had taken a dark turn for the worst. The two teenage princes had all but disappeared, leaving the throne in the evil hands of the scheming Queen Draxa. Some say the Queen murdered the King with a stealth dose of poison, drank with his favourite wine. Others say she put a memory spell on Ladon, the eldest prince, who now has absolutely no idea who he is and currently works as a server in the castle kitchen, waiting on Queen Draxa hand and foot. It is said Michaon, the youngest prince, fled for his life, his whereabouts unknown. The only hope for the people of Tora Island is for the young princes to raise an army, defeat the Queen, and claim back the throne. But as yet, there is only a sense of abandonment, and the momentary breath of peace, quickly turned into a deep, fearful sigh!

It is unnerving how the innocuous swishing and swaying of Queen Draxa's gown can instil a growing feeling of doom and trepidation amongst the courtiers. The chaffing of the raw silk material against itself and the floor was, indeed, the only sound to be heard as the Queen raged up and down the court. Prior to this, Queen Draxa had turned her bed chamber upside down looking for the missing item, normally secured in a bolted chest on her bedside table. Everything was turned out of its receptacle; papers and other objects rained down after their trajectory into the air. The four armed guards that stood in each corner of the room began to perspire under their armour, beads of anxious sweat trickled down their faces. The Queen was beyond angry and privy to the darkest magic ever to be known on Tora Island. There was no telling what she might do. Through gritted teeth, her face turning puce, she ordered the guards to fetch Bubo, her adviser and most trusted confidant. Seconds later his five feet, brown coloured wings entered the chamber, fanning everything in its wake with a cool breeze. Bubo had been incubated by a green parrot, thus giving him the ability to talk and his magic powers were a result of a genetic mutation. He had been King Leonex's adviser first and as the old monarch lay dying, he promised his master he would never abandon the kingdom and he kept his oath from the vantage point of Queen Draxa's shoulder.

"Bubo! The scroll has been stolen!" The Queen cried.

"Surely not?" He questioned, feigning surprise.

"Yes! Yes! Look!" She pointed to the empty chest hysterically, "someone has betrayed me and when I catch the culprit, I will send his measly bones to the four corners of this kingdom. Now summon the peasants! Someone must know something, and I will tighten the noose around this land until I get some answers. The scroll must be found because without it my reign is in jeopardy!"

"Yes, My Queen," said Bubo as a tingle of trepidation surged through his feathers, "straight away My Queen."

What horror was she going to unleash on the poor people of Tora Island? He only hoped they would have the strength to endure it.

A few moments later Queen Draxa swept onto the castle balcony and a great hush fell across the island. Its subjects looked at one another with wide eyed confusion as the Queen prepared to speak.

"A precious scroll has been taken from me and I intend to have it back! If the thief confesses now your families shall be spared!"

Deadly silence hung thick in the air. The Queen drew in a deep breath making her shoulders raise up, almost knocking Bubo off his perch.

"Very well," she announced ruthlessly, "you give me no choice!"

For a moment she surveyed her audience until her steely gaze fixed upon a small boy with a sweet, innocent face and angelic curls.

Oh goodness! What have I done? Thought Bubo to himself.

"Guards! Guards!" The Queen ordered, circling her long, bony index finger at the poor child, "take him to Deyjem!"

"No! No! Your Majesty!" The crowd cried and pleaded, the boy's parents sobbing uncontrollably.

The Queen projected her decree loudly across the almighty din of Tora's people.

"A child will be taken each day until my scroll is returned!" And with that, she exited the balcony with a powerful flourish.

CHAPTER THREE

I think there's someone following me?!

It was the day after the car boot sale and Maddie was awake early. She'd had an unusually bad night's sleep, her mom always said she slept the sleep of the dead and once even snored her way through the tail end of a hurricane. But last night was just plain weird. She dreamt of violent battles and ferocious beasts, tossing and turning from rest to wakefulness. At one point in the night, she even thought she saw some sort of big bird staring in through her window, its piercing eyes seemed to be locked into hers. She put her feather pillow over her head in frustration and redeemed the last vestiges of sleep until the alarm clock sounded its drill for the day to begin. She washed and dressed, and after breakfast gathered her schoolbooks, not forgetting the mysterious scroll, and met Jake at the bus stop.

"Hey!" Said Jake stuffing the last of a croissant into his mouth. At just twelve, Jake was big for his age with an appetite as large as his huge feet.

"Hey!" Maddie replied, stifling a yawn.

"Bad night?" Asked Jake.

"You could say that! Anyway Jake, about this scroll… meet me outside Mr. Peterson's art room at the end of the day, hopefully, he will be able to shed some light on our mystery."

"Our mystery Mads? You bought it!"

"Yea, whatever, just be there!" She was feeling a little crotchety due to the lack of sleep and felt relieved as the old, yellow and black bus groaned its way up the street, aligning right in front of her high tops. As the doors sprung open a strong, autumnal breeze whipped her hair in front of her face. She grabbed her wild mane with her free hand and momentarily glanced behind her.

Mmmmm... she thought to herself, the air, now still as a mill pond, *where did that come from?*

She shook her head and entered the vehicle, never before was she so grateful to collapse onto the worn out, leather seat. She rested her head on Jake's shoulder and promptly fell asleep. Moments later, screwed up paper balls started to rain down on their heads. It was the high schoolers sitting at the back of the bus.

"Hey Jakie! I'm tired too! Can you come over here and tuck me in? Whaa...."

They all pretended to cry like babies. If Jake were braver, he would tell them to shut up. The truth was he worried about going to high school. He could easily pass as a high schooler but inside, he still felt like a scared little kid. He decided to say nothing and listened instead as Maddie snored her way to school.

The day panned out in its usual fashion: first and second period, double math. Maddie could do a lot of things very well, but math was not one of them, she was always in the bottom group, much to Jakie's amusement! Third period was English, then lunch followed by social studies, science lab and finally art. For most of the day she dawdled her way from class to class, letting out a most unattractive yawn every so often.

"Jeez Maddie! I can almost see what you had for lunch," one of her classmates remarked.

"Funny," she replied, deadpan.

However, when the bell rang for sixth period, she suddenly got a surge of energy and whipped the scroll out of her locker and ran to find the art teacher, Mr. Peterson.

"Mr. Peterson! Mr. Peterson! I've got something really awesome to show you!" She blurted out excitedly.

He averted her eager gaze and continued to hand out papers as she danced around him like a puppy chasing a treat.

"Yes Madeline. Whatever it is it will have to wait until the end of class."

"But… but," she pleaded.

No buts Maddie, now take your seat.

Mr. Peterson had a soft spot for Maddie. She

was a really good kid and a very talented artist with great potential, but boy, she was so intense. He smiled to himself at her youthful eagerness.

Maddie watched the classroom clock as it slowly drew the school day to a close, each second excruciating, each minute another lesson in patience.

"Yes Maddie." Mr. Peterson said tidying up his desk, the last of the students chattering as they left the room.

"What is it that is so important? And you can tell Jake to come in. I can see him lurking in the doorway."

"I have something really cool to show you!" She said, promptly laying the scroll down flat on his desk, oblivious to the task he was in the middle of, and grabbed whatever objects were at hand to secure the corners.

"Tell me what you see? Go on... tell me what you see Mr. Peterson?"

There was that half smile again, her eyes widening with excitement.

"Well. It appears to be a portrait of a young

man, carrying a sword and wearing old fashioned clothes......"

"Yes, yes," she interrupted impatiently, "but look at his face!"

He hasn't got one, clearly Madeline.

"Exactly!" She agreed, mimicking her favourite super sleuth, "and that is the point!"

"Nothing you couldn't fix yourself Maddie," said Mr. Peterson underwhelmed.

"You think?"

She took a dramatic pause and then picked up a pencil from his desk and began to draw in the features. Mr. Peterson looked at Jake over the top of Maddie's head and rolled his eyes. He really didn't have time for this nonsense.

"There!" She said, pointing at the scroll.

"Well," said Mr. Peterson, "a fine attempt but I've seen you do better, now if you don't mind…"

"Watch!" She instructed and as he did so, the features seemed to disappear right in front of his eyes.

"How odd?" He queried, looking closely at the tip of the pencil, "It must be faulty, why don't you try another one."

"It doesn't make any difference, pencil, pen or paint, the face just keeps vanishing!"

Mr. Peterson opened his desk drawer, pulled out a large magnifying glass and proceeded to inspect the scroll.

"Curious" he said, "it is drawn on parchment and it appears to be rather old. Where did you get it from Maddie?"

"I bought it from Jake at the school fundraiser."

"And I got it from my grandma," Jake explained, "and she found it in the woods."

"Listen," Mr. Peterson said, "why don't I make a few phone calls and see if I can't get an antiquarian to examine it? Do you want to leave it with me Maddie?"

"No thanks Mr. Peterson. I feel like I need to keep hold of it."

"As you like. I'll see you tomorrow. Now

hurry or you'll miss your bus."

Jake and Maddie ran as fast as they could down the school hallway and out to their old faithful, black and yellow ride. The bus driver was just about to close the doors when Jake shouted for him to wait, waving his one free arm like crazy. He jumped on, greeted by the driver's glum looking face. Maddie was just about to hop on too when a strong gust of wind whipped her books from her arms. She frantically began to collect them, mouthing the word 'sorry' to the bus driver but he was impervious, his glum expression set in stone. The high schoolers, already picked up from their school, laughed and jeered at her as she struggled against the weighty breeze.

That's funny, Maddie thought to herself, *that's the second time today the autumn weather has pushed me about.*

She looked up to the sky and a cold shiver ran through her body.

The children decided to get off the bus a

couple of stops early. They often did this, after getting permission from their parents, to walk the tail end of the scenic route home. The detour passed through a park where they often sat idly on the swings or attempted a go on the monkey bars. Maddie was little for her age and not strong enough to hold her own weight, but Jake was pretty powerful.

"You know Jakie," declared Maddie, "If you just stood up to those high schoolers, they would leave us alone. You're much bigger and tougher than them already and you're only twelve."

She admired him as he traversed the length of the monkey bars.

"I don't want to talk about it Mads, okay?"

She knew by the expression on his face that he meant it, so she didn't pursue the conversation.

Suddenly, another huge gust of wind nearly blew Maddie off her swing. She pushed her long hair out of her face just in time to see a large, brown owl swoop down from the sky. As it settled onto a tree branch a few yards from them, the wind came to a sudden stop.

"Well, that's weird Jake."

"What is?"

"I thought owls were nocturnal?" She said pointing to the bird, who appeared to be staring right at them.

"Oh yea," exclaimed Jake, suddenly understanding the significance of what Maddie had said.

"It also looks a lot like the owl sitting outside my window last night. What's going on Jake?"

"I don't know Mads, but it looks as though we are going to find out. Maddie RUN!"

The great, majestic bird unfurled its huge wings, hovering for a second mid-air and flew directly towards the children. Maddie and Jake ran as fast as their legs could carry them, their hearts pounding, almost out of breath. Maddie was behind by a good length, when the scroll fell out of her backpack and onto the grass.

"No leave it Mads!" Shouted Jake, "It's not worth it!"

But Maddie was determined to retrieve her curious possession. Just as she picked it up the owl opened its ivory beak and locked on to the end of the scroll. Its beady eyes met hers as they both tussled to maintain ownership. Suddenly, Maddie felt a strange sensation growing in her hand and moving up her arm. The scroll was vibrating and glowing, an eerie green gold colour and, to her astonishment, her arm took on the same colour too! The bird immediately let go of the scroll and Maddie tumbled backwards onto the forgiving grass.

"Well, that changes the situation substantially!" Informed Bubo.

The children stared, dumbfounded, at the extraordinary talking owl. For the first time in her life, Maddie was speechless.

"It only lights up for its owner and that, my dear, appears to be you!"

It continued to stare, clearly perturbed, at Maddie.

"How did you come to possess the scroll young lady?"

Her mouth still agog, eyes widening, Maddie slowly looked at Jake for support and then back to the intimidating bird.

"Um... um...I...I... I bought it at the school fundraiser?"

Her answer sounded more like a question. The bird frightened her, and she didn't want to make it angry.

"So, coinage was exchanged?" It pushed for more details

"Do you mean money?" She queried

"Yes, yes, yes! Of course I mean money."

The bird ruffled its feathers in exasperation and both Maddie and Jake recoiled with fright. Bubo was not without feelings, and he could see the children were more than a little wary of him.

"I paid five dollars for it," offered Maddie.

"Then you are indeed the legitimate owner

of this magic scroll, and as such you now have responsibilities…"

"MAGIC!" Exclaimed Maddie, her face beaming with excitement. Bubo sighed to himself, he needed her to understand the gravity of the situation.

"I come from a parallel universe called Tora Island…"

"WHOA!" Maddie interrupted.

"Young Lady! I find your exuberance a little immature given the seriousness of our predicament."

"Sorry," she said as Bubo lifted his wing up to his beak and proffered a gentle, shush now.

"As I was saying, Tora Island is in the grip of the evil Queen Draxa, and this scroll here is the receptacle of the darkest magic. The portrait is of the heir to the throne, Prince Ladon. As you may have noticed, he has no face and thus, no memory of who he is. Until his features are drawn with the magic feather quill, he will remain a servant in the Queen's kitchen.

Unfortunately, we do not know where the quill is, but the scroll will guide us."

"What do you mean when you say, US?" Jake piped up.

"Well, me and the girl, of course. Because of her meddling she is now the owner of the scroll, and it will obey no one but her. She has to come back to Tora Island with me, the fate of the kingdom rests in her hands."

"WHAT!!" The friends exclaimed in sync.

"This is nuts!" Exploded Jake, "who and what kind of crazy bird are you?"

"My name is Bubo, and I am Queen Draxa's personal adviser. I am also the one who stole the scroll from her chamber. As long as the scroll and quill are separated, she will remain in power, unleashing her own personal brand of evil on my people. If Prince Ladon regains his memory he will fight, tooth and nail, to regain his throne. Please! You have no choice. Every day the scroll is missing she sends more children to the slave ship as punishment. You have to help me stop her!"

The children stared at one another, their eyes were wide with incomprehension, eyebrows dancing like a confused caterpillar.

"My mom would never allow it! Maddie explained, I have to be in bed by 9.00 o'clock."

"Me too!" Said Jake.

Bubo tried to bring some persuasive calm to the conversation and explained,

"We are going to a parallel universe and the time here will remain the same. When you come back it will be as though you have never left."

"IF we come back!" Said Jake, kicking the grass under his foot.

"Don't worry, I have magic too! It isn't as powerful as the Queens, but I will protect you."

Jake and Maddie formed a little huddle and whispered between themselves.

"Maddie, I have to be honest, this whole thing is more than a little scary and cuckoo!"

"But just think Jakie, if we can do this... standing up to the high schoolers will be a piece of cake. What do you think?"

Jake thought about it for a moment, rubbing his chin. He turned to face Bubo and said,

"Where Maddie goes, I go too! So how do we hitch a ride?"

Bubo paused for a moment with relief and then stretched out his large wings, blowing the children's hair back in the process.

"Hop on," he said with a wink.

And so, a series of events transpired to bring Maddie and Jake to this moment and to an adventure of a lifetime. And that, as they say, is … Cause and effect.

CHAPTER FOUR
What have we got ourselves into?

The lightning strike, as the threesome passed through the portal to Tora Island, seemed more surreal to Maddie than even the idea of a real, magic, talking owl. The all-encompassing white flash so confused her senses that she thought, with great relief, that this had all been a dream and she would wake up, with a well-rested stretch, in the comfort of her own bed. But alas, as the gentle heat from Tora's sunny island caressed her skin, she knew it was not a dream. She looked over at Jake, as they flew through the air, each holding onto a wing for dear life and could only anxiously imagine what lay ahead of them. Bubo landed near the camouflage of a large, leafy tree and told them to wait quietly while he went to gather provisions.

"Can you believe this Jake?" Said Maddie, with a mixture of excitement and trepidation.

"I'm trying hard not to Mads!" Jake replied, "I mean, this is ridiculous! The fate of a kingdom depending on US... US Madeline Forster and we're still wearing our school backpacks ready for tomorrow's double science class!"

Maddie didn't reply. Instead, they both sat quietly contemplating their fate and waited patiently for Bubo's return.

Bubo arrived a short while later clutching a variety of objects in his claws,

"Jake, here is a spear for you. There are plenty of fish to catch as you make your way around the coastline. Maddie, in this cloth bag is food and drink for your journey and a change of clothes so that you blend in with the locals."

Jake looked at Maddie confused and with increasing alarm,

"Hold on just one darn moment, why do you

keep referring to just to me and Maddie. You are coming with us, aren't you?"

Bubo paused for a moment before he divulged his plan,

"Jake, let me explain. The quill is made from one of my feathers; a precaution taken by the Queen to make sure her magic is more powerful. If I come with you, it will only confuse matters. Besides, I must stay with her otherwise she will become suspicious. Trust me, the further away you are, the safer you will be."

"TRUST YOU! TRUST YOU!" Exploded Jake, "You never said anything about us going by ourselves! We agreed to help YOU, not find the scroll solo! You said you would protect us!"

"And I will! I promise."

Bubo placed an elaborately decorated golden medallion around Maddie's neck, in its centre was an oval shaped, clear gemstone.

"Just rub it and we will be able to communicate. See!" Bubo explained, holding up a duplicate medallion he'd had hidden under his feathers, "it will be as though I'm with you."

"Oh, big whoop!" Said Jake sarcastically, "but you won't be, will you Bubo? And Maddie and I will have to face whatever is out there alone!"

"Jake," Maddie turned to face her old friend, grabbing both of his hands encouragingly, "we can do this!"

He sighed and shook his head, "Maddie, you've got me into some scrapes before but this... this is dangerous!"

"I know Jake. But I'm the legitimate owner of the scroll now and it won't energise for anyone else. I have no choice... but you do. I can't make you come with me."

But she could. He could never say no to his best friend.

The children changed clothes, Jake into a pair of rough, cotton trousers, long tabard and finished with a holster type belt for weapons. Maddie donned a white linen, draped dress which cinched her waist, flowing fully to her feet and picking up their backpacks, she carefully packed away their school outfits.

"Hey Jake! You look just like the picture on the scroll, except for the fact that you have a face."

Indeed, Jake did share more than a passing resemblance to Prince Ladon: his hair was the same blonde, worn slightly longer and textured looking. His tall, athletic build was a perfect match. If the prince had the same bright blue, intelligent looking eyes as Jake, they could easily be mistaken for brothers. He looked at Maddie, slightly taken aback by the newly gowned young lady before him. He was so used to seeing her in boyish jeans and high tops, that he was slightly flummoxed as to what to say. She'd even taken down her ponytail, letting her dark brown mane dance around her shoulders.

"Well?" She said expectantly, her green eyes eager for a compliment, what do you think?

"Ummm.... I... I... dunno," he said, all of a sudden embarrassed.

"You can hide your bags under this tree ready for your return home," Bubo suggested.

Jake let out a small, ironic laugh, "don't you mean IF we return home Bubo?"

Maddie shot Jake an imploring glance. They had to stay positive.

Bubo found a small patch of dirt and started to draw a map with his wing,

"Tora Island is a collection of coastal cities, a total of six, including Tora North, home to Queen Draxa, with the addition of two small land masses in the centre of the water surrounded by the peninsula. Follow the coastline west and go around the island: the quill must be hidden somewhere. Be careful who you trust, man or beast, it is hard to know who is loyal to our cause. Maddie, here is a leather container for the scroll: the strap will fit comfortably across your shoulders."

There was silence amongst the trio as the weight of the task weighed heavily upon them.

"Good luck," said Bubo, make haste and rest with the setting of the sun."

The children began to walk away when he

gave them some last, parting advice,

"Jake, you are braver than you think. And Maddie, try to stay calm and count to ten before you do anything rash."

A small nod of the head was confirmation that they understood the job at hand, and they walked westerly following the coastline.

CHAPTER FIVE
On the Road

A hand slowly released the leafy branch she had been spying through and it quickly bounced back to its usual form. It was the castle cook, Esmeralda. She had been gathering apples in a nearby orchard when she spotted the Queen's councillor, Bubo. She, like the rest of Tora's population, thought Bubo was steadfastly loyal to the evil monarch and was therefore wary of him. He was with a boy and a girl who were not locals. Esmeralda was too far away to hear what they were saying but she was concerned when they started to walk towards Tora Northwest. She would have to send a seagull messenger to the city and warn them of the strangers' arrival.

Meanwhile, Jake and Maddie were unusually

quiet as they started their journey. Every so often, they would turn and look at each other offering a brave smile. They took in the island landscape with its golden, sandy beaches, bright blue sky, and its lush greenery inland.

"It reminds me of Misquamicut Beach Jakie. Remember those colossal waves last summer? They were awesome!"

"Yea. Awesome Mads, really awesome."

There was a touch of sarcasm to Jake's voice, and Maddie felt really guilty that she'd got him involved in this mess.

"I should be having Taekwondo practice tonight."

"Don't worry Jake. Remember what Bubo said? The time will be just as we left it when we get back. So, you won't miss a thing."

"Yes, I remember what he said Maddie. The thing is, I just don't trust anything thing he says."

Maddie didn't want to say anything to Jake, but she was already a little homesick. Life was very different back in Connecticut. There was comfort in the certainty of each new day: school, friends, activities, home, and of course, Mom and Dad. She suddenly discovered a newly found appreciation of everything her parents did for her and now she had to look after herself and Jake... come what may. As she took in the views of Tora Island, she was amazed at how similar it looked to the coastline of Rhode Island. It gave her that warm, blue sky feeling. It made her want to stretch out like a contented cat and turn her face towards the sun. Under foot, were pebbles and larger stones which they had to navigate around. To their left, inland, grassy mounds worked their way up the island's hilly landscape. Pampas grass did a hula dance, prompted by a gentle breeze, and coconut trees dropped their fruit with a thuddy landing. To their right was the sea, showing off its dazzling horizon: heat rippling above the water, sunlight skipping on top of the waves and a perfect, ice blue sky. Above, Maddie could see a flock of seagulls flying westerly, the same direction as they were walking. They were so low she could almost see their faces; one bird had something tied around its neck. It reminded

Maddie of her uncle's racing pigeons.

That's strange, she said to herself and thought no more about it.

They had been walking in the heat of the day for what seemed like hours. In actual fact, it had only been an hour and a half, two at the most. They decided this would be a good time to rest under the shade of a tree and take in some much-needed refreshments. Maddie opened the cloth bag Bubo had given her and found some bread, cheese, apples, and a leather pouch filled with water.

"Here you go Jake," she handed him some food.

"Not exactly a double cheeseburger," he commiserated, but ate it with relish as he was starving

Whilst they were sitting, they noticed some funny little creatures a short distance away. They looked a bit like cats, but with the face of a raccoon. However, their posture was that of a small monkey with agile hind legs and capable hands. They seemed to be watching them, inching their little bottoms forward every so often.

"Look Jake. Aren't they cute!"

"Don't encourage them Mads. They could be dangerous!"

"Now you are being ridiculous. They look perfectly harmless......and probably a little hungry."

She held out a morsel of bread to tempt them and one fine specimen of the group ambled gingerly toward her.

"See! They are just looking for food."

The creature stretched out its arm and took the bread. It tentatively inspected Maddie, at first sniffing her, then touching the sleeve of her gown and pulling at her long, brown hair. Eventually, it sat boldly on her lap. Maddie was thrilled because she loved animals. It started to fiddle with the medallion around Maddie's neck, holding it up to its eye like a magnifying glass and then licking it.

"Oh Jake, isn't it funny."

"Be careful Mads, I don't trust it."

But before Maddie could scold him for being silly the sly thing whipped the medallion from her neck and ran off with it.

"Jake! The medallion! Run after it!"

In an instant Jake was on his feet and chasing after the creature. He was fast and strong, but the animal was a superior sprinter and before they knew it, the creature and its pack had disappeared, leaving a cloud of dust hanging in the air and two deflated kids.

"I told you not to encourage it, Maddie! Now what are we going to do? The medallion was our only source of communication with Bubo!"

"I'm so sorry Jake, I should have listened to you. Bubo told me to count to ten and think before I do anything rash, and now we are completely alone."

Jake could see her lip tremble as she tried hard not to cry.

"Don't worry Mads. I promise I will look after you." Jake gave his best friend a much-needed hug. "Come on. Let's grab our things and carry on. The sooner we find that quill the sooner we'll get home."

They proceeded with their coastal trek for a couple more hours before Jake decided it was time for a well-deserved break. He gestured for Maddie to come to the water's edge where he kicked off his shoes, rolled up his trousers and paddled to his knees.

"Come on Mads! It's nice and cool!"

Maddie didn't need to be asked twice. She threw her bag to the ground, released her eager feet by squashing the back of each shoe with its opposite and tied her long gown into a knot so it rested on her thigh.

"This is great!"

They splashed around for a little while and then sat down, side by side, on the soft, golden sand.

"Don't get too cosy Mads we need to make it to the first city before nightfall. It won't be long before the sun goes down and I don't know how cold it gets if we have to camp out."

Maddie rummaged about in the leather bag and pulled out two peaches.

"Here, eat this, you worry too much."

They both sat quietly admiring the island's seascape when they noticed a flash of light on the horizon. Slowly, slowly, a huge ship came into view. It looked unlike anything they had seen before. It was a sludge brown wooden vessel at least three stories high. It had an array of masts and flags with three lookout towers or crow's nests. At the front of the ship, the bow, were two ornate balconies. Peering out from the lower balcony was a gargantuan sized man. He was too far away to make out his features but, needless to say, his silhouette cast a sinister shadow. Above him appeared to be another person of normal stature but, without binoculars, it was impossible to glean any more detail. It was, all in all, a menacing looking craft.

"Mad?"

"Yea?"

"Do you see that light flashing?"

"Yea?"

"I'm not sure. But I think it might be some kind of signal, like an S.O.S."

"Do you think it might be the slave ship Bubo was telling us about?"

"Got it in one, Mads, and it looks like there are children captive on board."

"Oh no!" Maddie gasped the horror of Queen Draxa's evil appearing right before their eyes.

"Come on. We must find that quill. It's the only way to help them."

They gathered their belongings and continued with their quest. As they walked away, they were unaware of being watched by the gargantuan man.

A fiendish smile twisted across his ruddy face, as his colossal nose picked up the scent of the young strangers.

Mmmmm...... A heady aroma, he said to himself, smacking his lips in anticipation.

Maddie and Jake walked as far as their waning energy would take them.

Luckily for them, the day's heat kept them warm as they bedded down for the night under the protection of a lush tree and tall grass. They could see the fires and candlelight of a rambling city in the distance and decided they would venture there at first light.

CHAPTER SIX

Tora Northwest

Prince Michaon was the youngest son of the late King Leonex and the late Queen Prudenza. They had been a very happy family, not forgetting his older Brother and heir to the throne, Prince Ladon, until the passing of his mother and the subsequent marriage of Draxa to his father. The newly crowned Queen Draxa appeared all sweetness and light whilst they were courting but once the crown was on her head the two princes began to notice some worrying changes. They used to always eat their meals together at the grand table in the great banqueting hall. Then the Queen kept the once jolly king isolated from his family and friends, saying that he was ill and needed to rest.

The king used to walk among his people on a regular basis, asking them about their lives, their work, holding a small babe in his arms. But now he was never to be seen, and his subjects felt abandoned, as did his sons, by the once beloved King Leonex. Prince Ladon and Prince Michaon felt, for sure, there was something unearthly and evil about Queen Draxa, but they didn't know what. They used to see the Queen and her lady in waiting arguing furiously until one day they argued no more, and the maid seemed more compliant. It was around this time that the old king seemed to fall into a dangerously, deep sleep. So deep, in fact, that he consequently passed away without once regaining consciousness or saying goodbye to his sons. Prince Ladon was heartbroken and cried to his brother,

"I know what she has done! She is the devil!"

Prince Michaon didn't understand the implications of what his brother said until one day, not long after the poor king was buried, Michaon found Ladon wandering about the palace in a daze, seemingly with no knowledge of WHO or WHERE he was. He found him in the kitchens and tried to shake some sense into him but without any success. The kitchen cook, Esmeralda, grabbed the young prince and held him in a motherly embrace, advising him earnestly she said.

"Your Majesty, you have to leave this place. There is darkness at work here and in order to save Tora and its people from Queen Draxa, you must first save yourself. My son will accompany you to my family in Tora, Northwest, you'll be safe with them. Don't worry about your brother I will keep him by my side. Now go, the two of you, and God's speed to you."

And so, Prince Michaon found himself in Tora, Northwest, living with his man Servant, Jax and the cook's family. Jax was thirteen years old, the same age as the prince. He was as dark as the prince was blonde. His eyes glowed a bright amber and Michaon was more than grateful to have the loyalty which shone from his strong, likeable face. He was the only connection he had left to his life at the castle and although he could never replace Ladon, his brother, he thought of him as one and would forever be in his debt. They had received a message by carrier seagull the night before, warning them of strangers approaching the city so decided to stand guard in the market square ready for their arrival.

Maddie and Jake woke just as the sun was starting to rise. They had slept fitfully, given the fact that they had never been away from the comfort of their own beds, let alone slept under the stars in a foreign land! They were blurry eyed but sufficiently rested and had bread, cheese, and some cold water for breakfast. It wasn't long before they found themselves standing in front of the gated city, Tora, Northwest, ready to introduce themselves. Jake rapped his knuckles on the heavy, bolted door and waited for a reply. The friends looked at each other and both took a deep breath as the entrance slowly opened to reveal a busy, bustling marketplace. Vendors stood behind their stalls, people were milling about, either standing and chatting or bartering for fresh fruit, vegetables, and meat. There were dogs running about the place, cats hidden, high up on lofty beams, surveying the goings on from their superior vantage point. There was even a cow being milked and a beautiful, black horse being held steadfast by its reins. The inhabitants were dressed very similar to Jake and Maddie: the men wore trousers made of rough cotton with long tabards, and the women wore long, flowing gowns that draped gently across their bodies. Some of the men wore a skirt and cape, with a sword attached to their hip. It reminded Maddie of the Scottish kilt her Uncle Joe wore to family weddings. Two young men, who were wearing this particular attire, were staring right at them.

"Well?" Said an old woman at the gate, "are you buying or selling?"

"Huh?" Replied Jake, confused.

Maddie nudged him in the ribs, "buying," said Maddie quickly. She was better at thinking on her feet than Jake. Her mother always said she was a wylie cat and always kept one eye on her!

"Well," said the old woman grumpily, "you'd

better hurry up then, we're just about out of turnip bread."

"Turnip bread!" echoed Jake pulling a face. He was hungry but drew the line at vegetable bread. "Yuk!"

The woman pushed them roughly through, with a strength uncharacteristic in one so aged. Maddie lost her balance, tripping ungainly over her sandal clad feet. Regaining her composure, she lifted her head and found herself staring into a pair of startling blue eyes. Her stomach did a little flip and she seemed unable to utter a single syllable. The young man in the robe asked of her,

"Who are you? And what do you want at Tora, Northwest?"

"Uh... um... um... I... We."

Maddie was mute.

"I'm Jake and this is Maddie. We've travelled from Tora, North. We've come to buy at your market."

"You've travelled a long way," the young

man shot a glance at his dark-haired companion, "you must be tired. Come with us. We will find you a place to rest and eat. The market will trade all day."

The children didn't know how they were going to find the magic quill, only that they were to travel westerly around the island to search for it, so taking advantage of some home-grown hospitality seemed as good an idea as any. They followed the two young men out of the market square, down a narrow, winding alley, until they came upon a modest fisherman's cottage. The young blonde man opened the door and gestured them into one living space where the occupants ate or slept and simmering gently on a large, open fireplace was a delicious pot of grub. The room itself was dimly lit, and it took a couple of seconds for Jake and Maddie to adjust their eyes to the light. It was in that short space of time they found themselves surrounded by the two young men, and small group of older men and women, looking not in the least bit hospitable. This didn't bode well.

The young men raised their swords, "Now you can tell us what you are really doing here?"

"We told you already. We are here to buy goods from the market," Jake tried to sound convincing, but his shallow breathing betrayed his true feelings. He was scared.

"LIAR!" The young man with the blonde hair screamed at him and pushed Jake to the floor.

"Maybe your companion will be more obliging," and he grabbed Maddie forcefully, twisting her wrist.

"Owwwww!" She cried with pain.

Seeing his friend being hurt made Jake's blood boil!

"Hey! You leave her alone!" he shouted.

Jake jumped up and wrestled her away from her captor, then found himself fighting and grappling with his opponent on the dirt floor. He wished he was home.

"Stop it! Stop it!" Maddie screeched, but the other young man held her tight, and she could do nothing to help her friend.

Jake was face down on the ground; his arms pulled behind his back.

"Now, if you don't tell me who you are and why you are here, I swear I will break your bones! I know you are working for that miscreant, Bubo, the Queen's loyal advisor, so spill... do you hear me!"

"He's not! He's not!" Maddie cried.

The young blonde-haired man turned to look at her, still pinning Jake to the floor.

"He's not what?" he demanded, "you were both seen plotting with Bubo!"

"Yes... but... but... Bubo isn't..."

"Isn't what?" He demanded again; his patience visibly stretched.

"LOYAL! LOYAL! He isn't loyal to the Queen."

Maddie could see Jake shake his head in despair. She had given Bubo up at the first sign of trouble and to whom? Bubo was their only way out of this place and now she had placed him in jeopardy. She could see that Jake was disappointed, but what was she meant to do? Let Jake be beaten senseless?

"What do mean, Bubo isn't loyal to the Queen. He is her most trusted advisor."

Maddie paused for a moment, glancing briefly at Jake before replying.

"Let him go and I will tell you everything. First, I need to know that we can trust you. Lives are at stake here."

"Well, how do I know we can trust YOU!" The young blonde-haired man retorted.

"Well… you can't, we can't. I guess I will just have to go with my gut instinct which tells me we are on the same side. And you?"

His captor thought for a moment and then let Jake go. He held out his hand and helped him up from the floor.

After Jake dusted himself down, with Maddie at his side, they proceeded to tell their story. They started with the dim and distant bake sale back in America and the crazy plan for them to find the magic quill. After relaying all the details they could think of, they ended their tale with the theft of Bubo's medallion which was the only source of communication they had to him.

After what seemed a very lengthy pause the blonde-haired young man processed this new information, rubbing his chin with his index finger,

"So, let me get this straight. Bubo is, in fact, loyal to the old king and his heirs and has sent you," pointing directly at Maddie, "as the rightful owner of the scroll, to reunite it with the magic quill and restore order to Tora?"

Maddie and Jake nodded in unison.

"Very well then. Allow me to introduce myself. I am Prince Michaon, second in line to the throne of Tora Island."

He bowed with great flair and Maddie thought she was literally going to faint.

CHAPTER SEVEN
In the beginning

For two hundred years King Leonex and his ancestors were the kind rulers of Tora Island. The island experienced a peace and calm never known to its people before. Prior to this, Tora was a dark and dismal place, controlled by six evil witches, one for each of the main cities. The dark witch, Hec ruled Tora North protected by her ogre, Seygarth. Her sister witches ruled the other cities, each with their own ogre for protection. They worked the people hard, toiling the earth and fishing the sea. The ancient Tora people prayed to the sacred bull, but the witches made the people fight them to the death in a gladiatorial arena. It was a sad day when either the mighty beast or one of Tora's men lay slain on the dusty ground. The witches were a blood thirsty clan. For many years Tora's people endured their miserable existence under the rule of the witches until, one day, King Leonex's grandfather, four times removed, led an uprising which destroyed their oppressors, not with weapons, but with plain water! Battle after battle was lost to the old hags and Tora's people were punished mercilessly for their arrogance. The witches cackled together as they watched their serfs try to outwit them. Until one day, the old hag, Hec, wandered away from her giant and found herself in the grounds of Tora North castle, when a young serving maid threw out a bucket of dirty water from the balcony above and not knowing the witch was below, drenched her. Hec let out a spine curdling cry and proceeded to melt right in front of her subjects! King Leonex's grandfather, four times removed, sent word to the other cities as to how to defeat the witches and then brought a sacred bull to trample Hec's remains into the ground. The giants ran for the hills and lived out their lives in freedom, no longer having to protect the evil clan. And thus, peace and calm ensued for several generations, until one evening, two hundred years later, a fierce storm raged over the island. A bolt of lightning, full of magical energy, cracked the ground where Hec's remains lay entombed and slowly, slowly, her body parts reformed and the old hag sat up, an eerie grin, full of mischief, appeared on her craggy face.

Meanwhile, back at Tora North, Queen Draxa is sitting at her dressing table, admiring her reflection in the mirror. She takes her long, bony finger and traces it along her high cheekbones, down her fine, slim nose and around her coal black eyes. She likes this mask best of all. It was, after all, the face that bewitched the late King Leonex and gave her back her kingdom, albeit without her sisters, their void adding to the pleasure she took in punishing Tora's people. She opens a drawer to reveal half a dozen more magic masks, each with a different face and identity to give her the freedom to roam Tora without drawing attention to herself. She briefly takes off her Queen Draxa mask to reveal the old, old witch, Hec.

"Someone is trying to steal my throne, my

sisters. But I swear, on your sacred memories, I will send every scrawny child to the slave ship if my scroll is not returned!" Declared Hec, her wizened skin becoming more shrivelled as her face contorted with anger and frustration.

Using its magic, she placed Queen Draxa's face over hers and yelled for Bubo.

"Bubo! Bubo! Come here quickly"!

Bubo was going through important state papers when he heard the Queen scream from her chambers. Her voice always sent a chill down his spine, but more so recently, because of the part he played in the scroll's disappearance. He flew as quickly as his wings would take him and landed, promptly at her feet.

"Yes, my Queen," he enquired, "what can I do for you?"

"What you can do for me Bubo is find my scroll!"

"We are doing all that we can, my Queen, but as yet we have no leads as to its whereabouts," he explained, waiting for her to erupt.

"Not good enough! Tell the people to gather

under the castle balcony when the town clock strikes midday. Tell them each day the scroll is missing we will multiply the number of children sent to the slave ship. Send messenger seagulls to Deyjam and Keirs and tell them they must be on their guard. We have a traitor in our midst. Also, I want you personally to chaperone that fool, Prince Ladon to the castle tower. I want him under lock and key at all times. If anything happens to him, I will hold you accountable. He must never be allowed to regain his memory and, until my scroll is found, is to be watched night and day. That is all Bubo. Leave me."

Bubo was about to take his leave, shuffling slowly backwards towards the door, never turning his back on the monarch, as was the custom, when the queen motioned for him to stop.

"Oh, and Bubo," said the Queen as she continued to marvel at her beauty and with not an ounce of remorse she instructed him thus, "When you take the children from their parents, I don't want to hear any of their wailing or simpering... make sure you close the door on the way out!"

"Yes, my Queen," he said, slowing shutting the door, his wing trembling with trepidation as he did so.

CHAPTER EIGHT

Comrades

"There is nothing else for it!" Exclaimed, Prince Michaon, as he handed Maddie and Jake a wooden beaker filled with warm milk. "We are coming with you!"

The children looked at each other with an equal measure of confusion and disbelief.

"Jax and I will be your guide and protectors. Goodness knows you seem unable to defend yourselves and there are many dangers that come with our island life. Most importantly though, my brother is the rightful heir to Tora's throne, and it is my duty to see that his destiny is fulfilled. Just as it yours, Maddie Forster from...?"

"South Windsor, I believe it was, your Majesty," Jax intervened.

"Actually, Connecticut. South Windsor, Connecticut," corrected Maddie.

"......and don't forget the good old U.S of A., PLANET EARTH!" Added Jake grumpily,

Maddie looked at him in disbelief! They finally had some real help in their quest and Jake acts all insulted!

He must be hungry, she thought to herself, *it's been a long day and he always gets bad tempered when he's hungry.*

The four young people, allies in their quest, sat around a wooden table close to the fireplace. An older lady, one might presume to be Jax's Auntie served them each a bowl of grub with a basket of turnip bread. The grub turned out to be a tasty stew of meat and potatoes and the bread was more delicious than Maddie or Jake anticipated. They ate it with gusto.

"Does anyone want this last piece of bread?" Jake asked hopefully.

"No. No thank you, you eat it," the group answered in unison.

Jake's face lit up with delight as he stuffed the last morsel into his mouth. He was in a much better mood now that his appetite had been satisfied.

"Good. We shall leave in the morning," the prince announced, "You have the scroll in a safe place Maddie?"

The prince looked at her questioningly and Maddie confirmed with a nod of her head.

"Then tomorrow the scroll will guide us on our journey to take back the throne. Get some rest. We start out at first light."

The next morning, the four companions crept stealthily through the sleeping streets, as they made their way to the market square and the gated entrance. Jax's Auntie had prepared them a bag of food and drink which he carried on his back. Both he and the prince were experienced hunters, so they would not go hungry in any case. Once outside the gated city and into the vastness of Tora's beautiful landscape, the prince asked to see the scroll which he unrolled carefully to see the faceless portrait of his brother, king in waiting, Prince Ladon. Prince Michaon was clearly moved by this sight and his hands trembled as he held his brother's likeness. Maddie gently took the scroll from him and held it in the air. The scroll began to energise, sending a florescent glow through Maddie's arm and hand.

"This way! South westerly!" She exclaimed, reassured by the scroll's steady pull.

CHAPTER NINE
Nanny

Back in the day, when old King Leonex and his future wife Queen Prudenza were courting, the only way her father could bear to part with her was if her Nanny of old went with her. And so, when they were eventually married, Nanny came with them to Tora North. Nanny had looked after Queen Prudenza as a child, and she loved her as if she were her own. When the two Princes came along, she was there at each birth, each first word, and each first step. Life was blissful for a long while until Queen Prudenza became ill and died shortly afterward. Her charges were distraught without a mother or a wife, and so, when the king later married Draxa, it seemed as though a second chance at happiness had been found. Nanny became Draxa's maid and although, on the surface, all appeared cordial, there was something about Queen Draxa that made Nanny shudder. One day, Nanny entered Queen Draxa's bed chamber carrying freshly laundered linens and stopped dead in her tracks as she witnessed Draxa taking off her magic mask to reveal the true identity of the old witch, Hec.

"Oh no!" Nanny gasped in horror and revulsion, "I am going to get the King!"

"I wouldn't do that if I were you, my dear, not if you know what's good for you!"

"You can't stop me, you ungodly creature!"

"Well! We shall see about that!"

Hec conjured a wicked spell that split Nanny into two people. The interfering, do-gooder Nanny was sent swiftly to Deyjam's slave ship where she was entombed in its timbers, with only her gentle face to be seen looking out across the breadths of the sea. The bad Nanny, the one that can be tempted, as we all can, stayed by Hec's side to do her evil bidding. Bad nanny was as villainous as her mistress and followed her every movement like a loyal but misguided lap dog. Bubo recognised the scent of her badness but could not put a feather on it. It was only after the old king died that the wretched pair flaunted their vile natures. Bubo and bad Nanny were instantly wary of each other, like two black cats vying for their territory: hackles raised, treading carefully but keeping a most watchful eye on the other.

CHAPTER TEN

Hunting and Gathering

Maddie, Jake, Prince Michaon and Jax followed the coastline, walking close to the water's edge as they made their way towards the southwest of the island.

"If we carry on this way, my lord, we will doubtless come upon the city of Tora, Middle West," informed Jax, his eyes as serious as they were dark.

"Yes. Thank you, Jax. I am aware of that, but we have a long way to go until that point and we don't know what perils we may encounter as we progress."

Their eyes met for a moment and they both glanced behind them to where Maddie and Jake were dawdling at their coat tails. There was hardly any age gap between all four of them, but in terms of life experiences, Tora's newly acquired visitors and, more importantly, its saviours were no more equipped for this quest than a couple of babbling babies. Neither the prince nor Jax uttered any misgivings but were determined to help find the magic quill for Tora's sake, come what may.

Prince Michaon's casual conversation belied his true feelings about their impending journey when he asked Maddie and Jake,

"So… tell me about this America!"

They were both very homesick and the mere mention of it made their stomachs turn.

"It's the best place in the world!" Offered Jake, with relish.

"Steady there my friend, you might have more than just a little competition." The prince gave him a gentle smile, not in the least affronted.

"Well," explained Jake, "this time of year is

spectacular! People come from miles around just to see the colour of the autumn trees. We play for hours in the woods behind my grandma's house, don't we Mads?"

"Yea! That's where Jake's Grandma found the scroll! He took it to the rummage sale at school and I bought it! And voila! Said owner of the unfinished portrait at your service."

"And we will be eternally grateful to you both for putting yourselves in such peril to help save Tora and its people," offered the prince sincerely.

"We didn't have much of a choice!" stated Jake grumpily.

Uh oh, thought Maddie, someone's hungry. "Have we got any food?" She asked hopefully.

Jax, a young man of few words and a very brooding look said,

"A small amount of bread and cheese, not enough for four of us. We must hunt. You can help me," he said pointing at Jake.

"Me... but... but... I don't know how

to…" he stuttered.

"Of course, you could always stay and PLAY with Maddie?"

His tone of voice reminded Jake of the older kids on the school bus, and he could feel the anger building up inside of him.

"Lead the way!" He said to Jax, prompting him to go with his outstretched arm. He would show him! He wasn't some little baby!

Prince Michaon and Maddie remained and began to set up a small camp.

"It won't be long before we lose the light, and we don't want to be on foot in the dark. We'll rest here and start out first thing. Come, help me gather some driftwood for a fire. Jax and Jake will have to go inland into the forest to find food; they could be a while."

As they walked along the shoreline, there was a moment of complete peace. The sun was slowly setting, and the wind blew a caressing breeze on them both. Maddie bent down to pick up a wizened old piece of wood just as the prince did the same. Their touch was like an electric shock.

"Oh! Sorry," said Maddie.

"No. Take it," said the prince flustered, "it's yours."

"Not mine exactly. For the fire, remember?"

"Of course."

There was an awkward silence between them before they both laughed and shook their heads.

"I'm sorry about Jax, Maddie. My people have had it tough here on Tora Island. There hasn't been a lot of play for anyone, least of all children, Jax especially. He feels very responsible for me and takes his duty very seriously. He had to leave his family to protect me; I hope Jake will forgive his manner."

"Of course," she replied, "he just reminded me of our friendly neighbourhood bully. I could see that Jake felt it too."

"I'm sorry to hear that, Maddie. You know, if you stand up to a bully they soon back down."

"Are you going to stand up to the Queen?" She asked.

"Yes. When the time is right.......... For both me and Jake. You have to know when to pick your battle."

Jake and Jax were deep in the forest. They seemed to be walking for ages when suddenly, Jax's pace slowed to a creep. He turned to look at Jake, putting his index finger to his lips,

"Shhh!"

He moved a bit like Smokey, Jake's cat, when she was about to catch a mouse. He stopped for a moment, bending down to touch a set of small tracks in the earth. He sniffed the scent from his fingers and whispered,

"They're fresh! Come on!"

Jax handed Jake a knife and then took his bow from his shoulder and loaded it with an arrow. Jake gulped quietly thinking how much trouble he would be in if his mother saw him with this knife! In the distance, a group of wild pigs were foraging in the undergrowth. They grunted happily and were completely unaware of the boys' presence, for which Jake was grateful. He had never killed any living thing for food, the closest he had ever got to hunting and gathering was going to the supermarket with his mom, but he was hungry, they all were. His hand shook, and his breathing quickened at the thought of the task ahead.

"I will take out the smallest," Jax whispered, "it will be enough for four."

He took aim and his arrow flew through the air, hitting its target with quick precision. The rest of the herd squealed with fright and ran off into the woods.

"You can fetch it," instructed Jax.

"What?!" Exclaimed, Jake.

"I take it that's a NO to your share of roasted pork then?" Jax asked sarcastically.

Jake paused for a moment, took a deep breath, and retrieved their supper.

Back at their camp, Prince Michaon and Maddie made a fire and sat quietly chatting; the sun was quickly fading, and darkness waited to envelope them. They were so engrossed in their conversation that they failed to notice the boys return; they seemed to appear from nowhere like two friendly ghosts.

The prince quickly stood up, jubilant,

"Jax! Jake! You have saved us from hunger. I can see we shall have a feast tonight!"

"My lord," Jax bowed his head respectfully.

"Jake," queried Maddie, "Are you ok?"

"I think I am going to be sick," he explained and took himself to the water's edge.

Jax huffed and puffed as he prepared the meat for roasting.

"What is it Jax," asked the prince, "what troubles you?"

"Him!" He shouted with frustration, pointing towards Jake who was still retching, "He does, my Lord, I think we should cut him loose."

"HEY!" Maddie confronted Jax, "he goes

where I go, and this quest goes nowhere without me!"

"She speaks the truth Jax," explained Prince Michaon, "she is the rightful owner of the scroll."

"But he is a weak link, My Lord, and scared of his own shadow. Even the girl has more spirit. I have a bad feeling that he will be our undoing."

"Then it is your duty, Jax, to turn into him a warrior. You can start tomorrow. That is an order."

"Yes Sire. I understand."

Jake returned to the group unaware that he had been the subject of so many misgivings. There was a heavy silence as they sat eating their supper.

CHAPTER ELEVEN

Chase me

Maddie slept heavily on her makeshift, grassy bed. Her eyes didn't open once until a warm beam of early morning sunshine caressed her cheeks. For an instant she thought she was home being gently woken from her slumber by her mother's soft kiss and coaxing words. Time to get up sleepy head, she would say, but Maddie knew from the huge expanse of blue sky above her that she was still on Tora Island. In the distance, she could hear voices and she sat up to see Jake and Jax sword fighting near the water's edge.

"What on earth?" She said out loud, not realising that the prince could hear. He was standing mid-way between her and the boys,

"He is teaching him how to fight, on my command. You can see he is a quick learner. No one will bully him now."

Jake turned, smiled, and waved at Maddie. Somehow, he looked quite different to her. He ran towards her, out of breath but looking elated.

"What do you think Mads?" Jax said he would train me to fight. I can't wait to get home and show those bullies a thing or two!"

He swung his sword in the air, mimicking Luke Skywalker with his lightsaber. Maddie was lost for words; his confidence seemed to be growing by the minute.

"Yes, that is all very well," said the prince, "but for you to get home we first must find the quill. Come on let's go; we mustn't leave a stone unturned."

The group gathered their belongings and set off towards Tora Middle West. The Prince and Maddie led the way with Jake and Jax bringing up the rear. Jax gave Jake a friendly slap on the back,

"We will make a warrior out of you yet"!

The morning's training session gave them each a newfound respect for the other and for the first time, they exchanged a smile.

They seemed to walk forever along the island's billowing shoreline and under a bright, blue sky, punctuated by delicate, cobweb clouds. Each walked quietly, absorbed in their own thoughts and fears until a splash of ice cold, salt spray roused them from their dark broodings. They changed positions with ease and without thinking, as though they were racing in slow motion. One minute Maddie was heading the troop and the boys were at the back. Next thing, she found herself dawdling and distracted by an unusual shell in the sand or a bird in the air and ended up lagging way behind. Every so often, Jake would turn around and smile at her and then, almost immediately, the prince would do the same.

Boys! Maddie thought, to herself, *are a bit hard to work out!*

"STOP!" Ordered, Jax, his arm outstretched, pointing ahead to as far as the eye could see.

"What is it Jax?" Asked the prince, "what can you see?"

"I don't know yet. But can you see the plumes of sand rising into the air? Something is disturbing it and it is coming our way!"

"What are we going to do?" Asked Maddie, alarmed.

"Jax," ordered the prince, "give Jake your extra sword. Maddie, get behind us. Stand three abreast, swords at the ready!"

The three young men formed a line in front of Maddie, she was after all, the only one the scroll would energise for. Jake could feel his breath quicken and they all exchanged a sidewards glance, not moving from their position. The dusty horizon appeared to grow legs and feet and was running towards them. The children were all scared in their own way but knew, in their hearts, this was the first of many battles to save Tora from the evil Queen Draxa. Suddenly, as the great plume drew closer, it began to clear to reveal a pack of strange, feline looking creatures. Their bodies like that of a cat, faces patterned a bit like a raccoon, and they moved with great speed like agile little monkeys. They came to a sudden stop, and all sat their little bottoms down right in front of the children.

"Hey Jake!" Cried Maddie, "they are the creatures that stole our medallion!"

"You're right! Look at that one right in the middle. He has the medallion around his neck!"

Sure enough, there was the gold medallion with its clear, oval gemstone glistening in the sun. From his position in the pack, one could hazard a guess that he was their leader. He seemed to be smiling at them, a small, enticing grimace.

"We have to get it. The medallion is our only connection to Bubo and our way home," said Jake imploringly.

"Move very slowly," ordered the prince, "we don't want to scare them away. This animal is a native to Tora and is called a skittish because it is very jumpy... and fast! On the count of three, everyone walk cautiously towards them. One, two three!"

The children took each step together and each time they did the pack of skittish would all move their little bottoms backwards. With one more step, they stood up like Meer cats and with another, they fled.

"Quick after them!" Shouted Jax and they all ran as fast as they could after the little rascals.

"Don't lose the leader! He has the medallion!" Added Maddie.

The children gave chase and the skittish led them inland, away from the coastline and into the wooded forest. The more they ran, the deeper into the leafy maze they found themselves. Every now and then, the skittish would stop and reveal themselves, almost as though they were encouraging the children to follow. Eventually, when they were all out of breath and couldn't run a second more, they found that they had stopped in front of a huge, sprawling tree. It was as wide as it was tall, its foliage stretching towards the islands farthest reaches.

"Good grief!" Declared Maddie, "I'm pooped!"

"So am I! Me too! Ditto!" Answered, the boys in unison.

"Oh no!" cried, Jake miserably, "we've lost him and the medallion. How are we ever to get home if we can't contact Bubo?"

"Jake! Be quiet!" Jax ordered in a loud whisper. He put his index finger up to his lips and pursed an inaudible Shush! Walking towards them, with the medallion hanging brazenly from his neck was the leader of the pack. He sat his little bottom right down in front of them and stared up as if to say, well, come on then!

"SALUTATIONS!" A huge voice bellowed its greeting to the children.

They all covered their ears from the din and Maddie exclaimed,

"What was that? Is it a storm?"

"WELL DONE OREO! YOU'VE BROUGHT ME VISITORS!"

The young people all gasped, and the boys

instinctively drew their swords toward the speaker.

"Who are you?" Demanded, the Prince.

"Why, I am Pitvas, eldest brother of the clan Seygarth."

"Are you an ogre?" Asked Maddie, she had read about mythical creatures like giants and ogres in school.

"Indeed, young lady, but I prefer the term vertically unchallenged!"

"And the rest!" Jake piped in.

Looking at the ogre's fleshy girth, he was in fact as wide as he was long.

"I beg of you," appealed the colossal beast, "could you release me from this blessed bramble prison. We are so deep into the forest that you are the only visitors I have ever had, and I fear that soon I shall become one with my jailer."

"It could be a trick, my lord," said Jax to the Prince, "he is one of THEM, like Deyjam, the slave ship owner."

"Deyjam?" Enquired Pitvas, "A slave ship owner?"

"Yes," explained the prince, "and each day the Queen is without her magic scroll more children are sent to their doomed fate."

"Oh no! That is unthinkable. My brother, Deyjam, is indeed under the queen's wicked spell of darkness."

"Sir.... Pitvas, I am Prince Michaon, second heir to the throne of Tora Island. My brother, Prince Ladon, is the rightful King of this land but Queen Draxa has relieved him of his memory with the use of this magic scroll."

Maddie presented the faceless image on the scroll to Pitvas, who shook his head in commiseration.

"We are on a quest to find the cure, the magic quill, to finish the portrait of Prince Ladon and restore his memory. Then with the rightful heir we can organise an army and take back the throne."

"Ah!" Said Pitvas, "I understand how you

feel. Not only has she hypnotised Deyjam to do her evil bidding, but also my brother, Kiers. My youngest brother, Weyo, like me, wasn't as easy to bewitch to her dark ways. So, she put a spell on him and now he wanders the island aimlessly singing, like the fool she turned him into. As for myself, I have been tied to this blasted tree ever since she married the old king, so much so, that I don't know where I end, and it begins!"

"But why Pitvas?" Asked the Prince, confused, "I understand her malice towards me and my brother but why has she done this to you and your kin?"

"A very good question, my Lord and one that will take time to explain," said Pitvas. "Do you think you could release me first?"

"Of course. It will be my pleasure," said the prince, "Jax, Jake... swords if you please."

The children beat back the strangle hold of branches but try as they might the tree would not relinquish its prey.

"This is useless!" Exclaimed Maddie, "we have the medallion, why don't we contact Bubo?

He'll know what to do."

They all exchanged eager glances, finally resting on Pitvas, who bellowed in a voice so loud the ground seemed to shudder,

"OREO! BRING ME THE MEDALLION!"

CHAPTER TWELVE

Suspicion

Back at the castle, Queen Draxa and her entourage were on the balcony addressing Tora's people once again. As she promised, every day the scroll remained at large, a poor child, and sometimes two, were taken to Deyjam and his slave ship. Tora's people were ignorant of the scroll's whereabouts and could only watch in despair as another little one was prized from its parent's grip. Rumours were rife and it didn't take long for the city to learn of Prince Ladon's imprisonment in the tower and, it was clear, their only hope of salvation was if Prince Michaon returned with an army and dethroned Queen Draxa. As usual, Bubo was perched on the Queen's shoulder, his loyal pretence becoming more difficult to stomach with each passing day. Suddenly, his medallion, which he kept hidden in the depths of his feathers, began to vibrate.

Thank goodness for that! He thought to himself. He had begun to fear for the children's safety. At least now he could be assured that they were alive and well and the quest for the magic quill still ongoing. He needed to take his leave of the Queen without causing too much fuss and whispered in her ear about some important papers that needed urgent attention. She flicked her hand at him, as though he were a repellent insect on her person and he hovered in the air, offering a small bow to her majesty before quitting her presence. He flew to his private lodgings within the castle and retrieved the medallion.

"Hello? Maddie, Jake? Are you there?"

Bubo rubbed the clear gemstone in the middle of the medallion, and it lit up revealing the children's faces, like looking into a crystal ball.

"Bubo!" Cried Maddie, "we're so happy to see you! We lost the medallion temporarily which is why we couldn't contact you."

"You must be more careful!" Bubo scolded them. "Where are you?"

The prince gestured to Maddie to give him the medallion and he said,

"We are inland, deep in the forest, we were on our way to Tora Middle West when were side-tracked."

"Your Majesty!" Exclaimed Bubo, surprised by the reflection staring back at him, "I am honoured and delighted to see you! How did you come upon Maddie and Jake?"

"We were made aware of their arrival and now myself and my man servant have joined the quest to find the quill. Master Bubo, how does my brother, Prince Ladon fare?"

"He is a prisoner in the tower, my Lord. The Queen is even more ruthless now the scroll is missing."

"Please watch over him until my return, I beg

of you."

"I will my Lord," promised Bubo.

"Tell him about Pitvas!" urged the others, to the prince.

"Bubo, we have come across the ogre, Pitvas. The Queen has imprisoned him in a tree. If we don't get him out, he will soon disappear forever beneath its gnarly branches. But it does not retreat, even with the sharpest of blades!"

"Ah! Yes. I know that particular species of tree. It will only contract and release its prey when hit with a certain cone shaped cactus plant. It grows freely in our island temperatures, especially deep in the forest where you are. The one you are looking for has a red bloom for danger. When you find it, chop it down and spear it with your sword. Hit the tree with it but no flesh, neither human nor ogre. It has a poisonous substance in its prickles. Dispose of it carefully your Majesty for there is no cure."

Suddenly, Bubo's voice took on more of a whisper.

"I have to go your Majesty. I think I can hear someone coming."

Bubo quickly plunged the medallion deep into his feather coat and opened his door to find bad nanny standing there with a suspicious look on her face.

"Ah! Madam Nanny," said Bubo, his voice as calm as a mill pond, "always a pleasure. Is there something I can help you with?"

"I was concerned for your wellbeing, Master Bubo, you left the Queen's presence in such a rush!" She explained slyly.

"I remembered I had some important papers to attend to. I hope you haven't been waiting long? I confess, I didn't hear you knock."

"Tut, tut, Master Bubo, confessions can wait, I was waiting but long enough...."

"Long enough, Madame Nanny, I don't understand?"

"Long enough to make sure you are alright and so I have. Shall we return to the proceedings?"

"Yes, of course. All matters are in hand," he said as he locked his door shut.

"So, it is Master Bubo, so it is," she replied with a forced smile, and they made their way down the long hallway back to the Queen.

Bubo was not overly concerned about bad nanny. The walls to the rooms were unusually thick, even with his own super, sensitive hearing, he would struggle to hear what was being said behind a closed door. All the same, he crossed his feathers and hoped that he was right.

CHAPTER THIRTEEN
Pitvas

Back in the forest, the children did as Bubo suggested and went on a hunt for the cone shaped cactus plant with a red bloom. Always the intrepid scout, Jax marked notches on the trees as they passed so they could find their way back to the captive, Pitvas. It wasn't long before Jake spied what they were looking for,

"Hey! Everyone! I think I've found it!" He yelled, excitedly.

"Well spotted Jake!" Said the prince and he quickly chopped it down.

"Look! There's another one!" Exclaimed Maddie, pointing ahead.

"Let me, my Lord," said Jax, quickly running off to retrieve the cactus.

Once they followed Jax's trail back to Pitvas, they began to bash the branches that entangled the huge ogre. Eventually, he was able to free his arms and then his legs until he fell, with a great thud, onto the ground, sending an explosion of dirt and leaves into the air as he did so.

"Oh! Thank you, my new friends, a million times thank you! I was afraid I would die in my leafy tomb!"

The ogre sat up and the skittishes jumped all over him, licking his face and squealing with delight.

"Ah! My babies! I love you too!"

For quite a few moments, Pitvas quite forgot himself and revelled in the reunion with his beloved pets, kissing and cuddling them. After a while, he felt the eyes of his saviours set squarely upon him.

"Umm…Yes. And so, to business," he said seriously.

As he stood up the ground beneath seemed to shake under his tremendous stature.

"Here, have some water," Maddie stood on her tiptoes, stretching her arm as she did so and handed Pitvas the leather crafted bottle.

"Such kindness," said the ogre, looking directly at Maddie, "Just a drop to moisten my tongue, if you please."

The container looked like a thimble in his enormous hand, and he drank the lot, for only a drop it was in his cavernous mouth.

"Why were you imprisoned in the tree Pitvas?" Asked Maddie, "You promised to tell us."

"Yes, Yes tell us Pitvas," chimed the rest of the children.

"My apologies, Your Majesty, I fear my story will only add to your woes."

"Just get on with it ogre," ordered Jax, frustrated. The rest of the group glared at him, shaking their heads.

"Hundreds of years ago the kingdom was

held in the grip of evil witches, all sisters. My clan, the ogres, fell under their wicked spell and were forced to do their bidding. The deposed king, your ancestor your majesty, slay the witches by some mysterious deed and the kingdom rejoiced, as did all ogres, for they awoke from their bewitching."

"What has this mumbo jumbo got to do with our quest?" Jake sided with Jax, for they were now true friends, "we haven't got time for this nonsense!"

"Patience, young sir."

The ogre bent down and looked Jake square in the eyes.

"Tis not nonsense; nor is it mumbo jumbo and has everything to do with your quest!"

"Hold your tongue Jake," demanded the prince, "Pitvas…please continue."

"Never have the ogres been so entranced… until now. The minute the old king, your father, announced his betrothal to Queen Draxa, everything changed. Somehow the Queen turned my brothers, Deyjam and Kiers, to her wicked ways and she locked me away in my forest prison. My youngest brother, Weyo, I believe just roams the island singing his favourite song. He has always been a simple soul and not much of a threat to anyone, especially the Queen."

"But why would she do this Pitvas?" Asked Maddie.

"Because she is not who we think she is, young Miss. Only the old witches could enchant an ogre so."

"You think she is a witch Pitvas?" Maddie's eyes opened wide with surprise.

"Yes, I do."

"I thought you said all the witches were dead?" Queried the prince.

"So I thought," Pitvas said gloomily.

"It would make sense," added Jake, "Bubo said she had very powerful magic. More powerful than anything he could muster."

"Pitvas," asked the prince, "do you know

how our ancestors defeated the witches?"

"No, your Majesty, I am sorry to say I don't."

"There must be a way to defeat Queen Draxa or whoever she is, my Lord," said Jax flourishing his sword.

"I hope you're right Jax, but for the moment we must concentrate on our quest. We must reunite the scroll and quill if we have any chance of raising an army and crowning my brother, Prince Ladon, king of Tora Island. So, if everyone is ready, we must make haste to Tora Mid-west. Pitvas, will you join us?

"It would be my honour, your Majesty." Turning to look at Maddie he added, "and how would you like a ride on my shoulders, young lady, tis a long road ahead."

Maddie beamed with delight and quickly climbed onto the ogre's back.

This is a first, she thought to herself, as she took in the beauty of Tora Island from her new vantage point.

The children set off towards their next

destination: the boys leading the way, Maddie and Pitvas behind, and the skittishes bringing up the rear, scouting for danger.

CHAPTER FOURTEEN

Bubo is in trouble

Bubo's distrust of bad Nanny was confirmed when the Queen's armed guard came to his chambers and insisted on escorting him to the throne room to see her. When they arrived, he was pushed forward, knocking him off his feet, then sliding along the marble floor until he came to a complete stop. Bubo gulped with fear and dread; this did not look good for him.

"Ah! Master Bubo," proclaimed the queen, "my loyal and trusted advisor!"

She forced a smile which quickly unravelled into a snarl.

"Up… up you get Master Bubo. We can't have you in a heap like an unwanted rag doll."

She raised her arms in front of her like a conductor preparing an orchestra.

"Your Majesty," replied Bubo as he struggled to his feet.

"That's better," the snarl returning to her lips.

"You summoned me, my Queen?"

"Yes… yes, such a silly notion Master Bubo but Nanny here," she pointed to bad Nanny standing by the side of the throne, a wide grin at home on her smug face, "thinks you are acting suspiciously, that you have something to hide. I told her it was impossible because you are my loyal and trusted advisor, but Nanny was so insistent and frankly, getting old and rather feeble, I felt inclined to indulge her. So…."

"Your Majesty?"

"Bubo! Do not toy with me! Have you something to hide?"

"No! Of course not, Your Highness."

"Then you won't mind if the guards search you," she nodded her head and her armed men circled him.

"Please! I must protest!"

Within seconds the guards rummaged deep into his feathers and brought out the medallion.

"Ah! What have we got here? Give it to me you imbeciles!" The queen shouted as she snatched the medallion from the guard's grip.

"See! I told you he was hiding something, my Queen," declared bad Nanny, "he makes my heckles rise, treacherous villain!"

"Do shut up Nanny!"

"'Tis nothing, Your Majesty. Just a small fancy, an heirloom left to me. It is of sentimental importance only."

The Queen held the medallion at arm's length, the clear gemstone glinting in a ray of sunlight from a nearby window.

"Such a pretty treasure, Master Bubo. I am surprised you have let it get so dusty. All it needs is a little polish and it will be perfectly restored."

The Queen and Bubo locked eyes for a moment. She enjoyed watching Bubo squirm.

"Nanny, bring me a dust cloth!"

"Yes, your Majesty."

Nanny found a small piece of soft cloth and handed it to the Queen who proceeded to rub the oval shaped gemstone. Immediately, the medallion began to vibrate.

"Well, well, well, Master Bubo what have we got here? Guards! Put him in the tower with that fool, Prince Ladon. Chain him tight until I decide what to do with him."

"Kill him! My Queen," piped bad Nanny.

"All in good time Nanny. He may come in useful yet. We must see what a little painful persuasion reveals."

"Pluck out all his feathers and dip him in oil ready for roasting!"

"Oh my precious Nanny. You do love your blood sports!" The Queen gave her a big hug, "which is why we make the perfect team!"

They both laughed out loud. The evil cackling seemed to bounce off the castle walls sending a message, to all who heard it, of impending doom.

CHAPTER FIFTEEN

Tora, Mid-west

The children and Pitvas walked most of the day, stopping for food and water infrequently, in an attempt to reach Tora Mid-west before sundown. They kept to plan and arrived with just enough daylight to see clearly. They knocked on the gate but to no avail; the village was as quiet as a mouse, and for all intents and purposes appeared deserted.

"Is anyone there?" Boomed Pitvas. There was no reply, just an unnerving silence, "Well that's odd, Tora Mid-west is a busy, bustling city; it is highly suspicious for it to be so ......"

Even before he could finish his sentence, they found themselves under attack. Men jumped from the parapets atop the high city walls, three of them landing on poor Pitvas who thrashed at them and then stumbled to the ground. Some of the attackers had swords and those without, had clubs or large sticks. It was lucky Jake had been schooled by Jax in hand-to-hand combat. They practiced every spare moment, and he was now very skilled in the ways of the blade. The fighting continued and Jake caught his opponent's arm with his sword.

"Ah!" He cried, blood pouring from the wound. The rest of his men stopped what they were doing, staring at him, transfixed.

"My fighting arm! You! You have rendered it useless!" The man stared at Jake with blind fury.

"It's hardly my fault," he replied, "you attacked us first!"

"Yes!" Added Prince Michaon, "for what reason I know not!"

"You were going to ransack the city; what other reason could there be?"

"We are not thieves or hooligans sir! I am

Prince Michaon, and we are on a quest to find the magic quill, unite it with the scroll and take back the throne from that usurper, Queen Draxa."

"……and the ogre?"

"He is our trusted companion."

"Your Majesty! Please forgive me, but I can assure you we have no quill in Tora Mid-west."

Maddie took the scroll from its container and held it in the air. It did not energise; the man was telling the truth. Suddenly, he let out a big groan, and clutching his arm he collapsed to the floor. One of his men came over and wrapped the wound with his own shirt.

"Marcellus, what are we going to do? You can't fight at the arena like this; there is no one to take your place!"

"Yes, there is," replied Marcellus, "Him!" He pointed directly at Jake, "he is the one that injured me and now he owes me a debt."

"What?!" The children cried in unison.

"We are due to fight the bulls in the arena. If we don't, the city and our people will be severely punished. I am the best fighter in Tora Midwest and now I have been injured, the victor must take my place. It is our way."

"It's not my way!" Retorted, Jake.

Marcellus started to turn a pale shade of grey, please, take me home. I need medical attention.

Everyone passed through the city gate, eventually arriving at a modest house. Once inside, the children were offered refreshments which they eagerly consumed. Pitvas sat outside because he was far too big for the home's small door frame and low ceilings. The host, Marcellus' wife, brought out sustenance for the old ogre, who accepted it graciously. He was, indeed, a truly gentle giant. Inside, they waited for the doctor to arrive.

"When are you due to fight at the arena Marcellus?" Asked, the Prince.

"Tomorrow at noon, Your Highness."

"It is a travesty and injustice that Queen

Draxa reintroduced these barbaric games."

"I agree, Your Majesty, but if we don't send a warrior our people will suffer."

"There is nothing else for it," declared the prince, "I will fight in the arena."

"No! Sire! You can't!" Exclaimed Jax, "You are the second heir to the throne. What if Prince Ladon never regains his memory?"

"But he will Jax!"

"But if he doesn't sire......you will be king. We cannot take the risk."

"He owes me a debt," Marcellus pointed at Jake, "it must be him!"

"No!" Maddie cried, with terror.

Jake comforted her and wrapping his arms around her said, "don't worry Maddie, Jax has taught me well. I am ready."

He looked around the room, a new steely determination glinting in his eyes. The silence that hung thick in the air spoke volumes as to the enormity of the task and all that could be heard was the muffled whimpers as Maddie snuggled her head into Jake's chest.

"We will leave tomorrow at first light," ordered the prince, "Jake, get some rest. You will need every ounce of strength and energy to fight the bulls. May the gods protect you."

CHAPTER SIXTEEN

The Arena

The next morning, the children and Pitvas gathered outside the city gates preparing to leave. Marcellus, with his bandaged arm, offered some last-minute advice.

"The arena is on the opposite side of the island. You will have to cross it by sea. There are two small boats with supplies moored by the shore; two of my men will accompany you. They will know what to do when you get there."

"Thank you," said the prince.

Marcellus turned and looked at Jake.

"Good luck young warrior. The city salutes you."

He patted Jake on the shoulder with his good hand and retreated back behind the city gates.

"Your Majesty," said Pitvas, "I think it best if I take my leave…"

"What?! No!!," Maddie interrupted.

"Not permanently young lady. I will never fit into a small boat for starters, but, more importantly, I cannot take the chance that Deyjam might sense my presence. There is time enough for that later. I am going to find my brother, Weyo, in Tora, Northeast. As I said before, he is a simple soul but very strong, and we will meet you at Tora South. If the quill is anywhere, I believe it will be there, with my brother, Kiers."

"Agreed," said the prince.

"But first, I have a parting gift for Jake."

He handed Jake a parcel wrapped in thick cloth.

"It is the cactus plant you freed me with. I thought it might come in handy. Spear it with your sword when you come to fight the bulls. It is your best chance."

"Thank you, Pitvas. I will do just that."

"Until we meet again my friends!"'

The old ogre called for his skittishes and slowly walked away, the ground grumbling under his feet, an explosion of dust dancing in the air with each step.

The children and the two men boarded the boats and sailed from Tora, Mid-west to Arena City. They passed two small land masses which Deyjam's slave ship used as a mooring, but he thankfully was nowhere to be seen. Arriving at their destination half an hour before the games commenced, they tied the vessels to the pier and stopped for a moment to take in the hustle and bustle playing out in front of them. The actual arena, which looked very like an old roman amphitheatre, took centre stage with the rest of the city sprawled out around it. There were fishermen bringing in their morning catch, traders exchanging wares in the local market, and women with their babes chatting and playing in the sunshine. However, the sight that sent a shiver down the spine of the children, was that of fighters sharpening their swords and other weapons in the market square. After they crafted them into the sharpest point, they held them in the air to inspect their work and the glare of the sun bounced off the metal, momentarily blinding the children as they watched. No one said a word until one of the men that had accompanied their party motioned for them to follow.

"This way to the arena. We need to take you to the Master of Ceremonies before the games begin."

They made their way silently through the crowded streets, each absorbed in their own thoughts, trying to make sense of the situation they now found themselves in. Maddie and Jake's eyes locked together for what seemed an eternity, but in reality, was just a minute or so. Why oh why had they agreed to this crazy quest? They could be at home, in Connecticut, playing basketball in Jake's front yard or sitting in Maddie's tree house, taking in the glory of a New England fall. Instead, they were here, on

Tora Island, fighting a fight that wasn't theirs and now Jake's life was in serious jeopardy. After a short walk they entered the amphitheatre. It was a dark, dank building made of large, grey stone and water trickled down the walls where mildew spawned at every crevice. They were walking through a hallway that circled the arena and its design enabled them to see the stage and the gathering audience. To their rear were dirt floor rooms with wrought iron caged doors; it reminded Maddie of the jail cells in old western movies. Finally, they arrived at a much bigger room which boasted some basic comforts: a bed, a table, and a large wooden chair on which sat an equally large man. The children assumed rightly that he was the Master of Ceremonies. He was dressed in plated armour which covered his chest and his legs. Maddie and Jake had seen historical costume like this in their schoolbooks, but it was the two large bull horns protruding from his helmet that caught their gaze.

"Ah!" He said, in a deep booming voice, "magnificent, aren't they? They are a trophy from the very first games Queen Draxa reinstated."

Maddie's lips curled in disgust: first for the fate of the poor animal relieved of it horns, second because the Master of ceremonies seemed to hold his patron, Queen Draxa in such high esteem. She felt sick to her stomach when she thought of the task ahead and grabbed Jake's hand.

The man who had led them here approached the Master of Ceremonies.

"Sir, Marcellus from Tora Mid-west is injured. He has sent this young warrior in his stead."

"Ah! Has he now?"

"If it pleases you, Sir?"

"Well, let's take a look."

With that, he sauntered over to Jake, circled him once and then with his index finger tilted his chin backwards for further inspection.

"Where are you from boy?"

"Um... um... Connecticut."

"Con…nect…icut? Never heard of it."

"A foreign land sir," interjected the prince, "he is here to take in the sights."

The Master of Ceremonies paused for a moment and then with a big grin exclaimed,

"Ah! Yes! That will do nicely. A foreigner prepared to die for our Queen. I shall get a knighthood for sure! Ready yourself young warrior for I must take my leave; the audience awaits!"

With that, he exited the room and made his way to the centre of the arena. The children could hear the noise of the crowd, it sounded less like cheering and more like a huge moaning. Not one citizen really wanted to be there, but were forced to endure this barbaric spectacle by Draxa, their sadistic ruler.

"Your Majesty," their guide said, "I must get back to Tora, Mid-west. We will leave a boat for you and your party, should you need it. I will pray for the success of your quest, and I will pray for you, young sir."

He paused for a moment, enveloping Jake in

a fatherly hug, after which he quickly disappeared.

The children all stared at each other, fear and trepidation written over each of their faces. Suddenly, they heard the Master of Ceremonies' booming voice,

"Contestants all! Come and meet your adoring fans!"

"No Jake......Please! You don't have to do this. I just want to go home."

Maddie started to cry.

"Don't cry Mads. We have to finish what we've started and then Bubo will fly us back to South Windsor, back to the very same place and time, remember?"

Maddie couldn't speak. She nodded her head through a stream of tears: huge sobs escaped her mouth, although she tried with all her might to hold them back. Jake hugged her tight and then they made their way towards the arena and towards the sound of the awaiting crowd. Jake and the other two contestants walked into the centre of the arena stage and the Master of

Ceremonies encouraged the audience to cheer. All the children could do was to wait in the wings and anxiously watch the events unfold. He swaggered around the stage, preening and primping like a colourful ostrich, and after his ego had bathed in a sufficient amount of adoration, he introduced the contestants.

"... and finally, we have Jake from the foreign land of Conn...conn..."

The Master of ceremonies struggled to pronounce the word and eventually, Jake shouted it as loudly and proudly as he could,

"CONNECTICUT, U.S.A!"

The audience applauded and the first fighter took his place ready for the games to begin. Jake and the other man waited in the wings with the others.

"Warriors!" The Master of Ceremonies exclaimed, "it is a good day to die!"

Suddenly, a quiet hush rippled through the audience as the gate enclosing the bull was opened, revealing a beast of monstrous proportions. It had two enormous horns that twirled skywards, protruding from an equally large head. Its glossy black coat wrapped itself around a formidable girth and set of muscles. Stomping its hooves, which glinted in the sunlight, almost as if they were made of some precious metal, the animal breathed deeply and moaned as it foraged fruitlessly in the dirt floor, oblivious to the waiting crowd. It glanced up and caught sight of the awaiting matador and instantly, its hackles rose, thrusting its chest and flaring its huge nostrils. All eyes were on the poor man, forced to battle with the creature, who stood terrified and was visibly shaking. Suddenly, the animal let out a ferocious bellow and began to charge. The man froze with fear and in an instant his fate was sealed as he was skewered onto the beast's horn. Back in the wings Maddie swooned and was steadied by the prince, as Jax put a comforting arm around Jake's shoulder. The second warrior entered the stage determined to put up a fight and the spectators held their breath as he readied his sword in front of him. Once again, the bull charged at the man with all of its might, head down, horns ready to gouge its victim. However, this time the fighter was quicker on his feet, and he managed to swerve out of the animal's way stabbing it deeply as he did so. The bull roared in pain and walked away, circling around itself in anguish. The children and the audience hoped that the injury would put the beast off, but defiantly, it charged again and this time it didn't fail. The Master of Ceremonies called for the final warrior to take to the stage. Jake breathed deeply and took one final look at his best friend, Maddie, whose face was sodden with tears. He forced one foot in front of the other but, as he did so, he felt a hand push him backwards out of the way. Before he knew what was happening, Jax was in the arena in his place.

"This is most uncommon!" Said the Master of Ceremonies, "but equally exciting! Proceed warrior!"

The bull stomped at the ground, bellowing loudly, and breathing heavily through flared nostrils. Jax took up his fighting stance and prepared himself for the animal to charge. The adrenaline was racing through his body, all of his senses on high alert.

The bull charged at Jax but, luckily, the injury it had sustained earlier slowed the animal down somewhat and he jumped out of the way, piercing it again with his sword as he did so. The animal cried in pain and anger, all the more determined to stop its tormentor. The beast pressed forward at a ferocious pace and chased Jax around the arena. Jax baited the bull to keep running, in an attempt to tire the animal out, but despite its wounds it carried on relentless. Jax was out of breath, his body fatigued, and in a split second he felt horns lift him off of the ground, throwing him into the air only to land with a loud thud on the ground. The audience gasped with horror at the inevitable scene to be played out whilst Jake, back in the wings, retrieved the cactus plant Pitvas had given him and carefully pierced it onto his sword.

"Jake!" Cried Maddie, "What are you doing?"

"I have to help him Mads. He's my friend."

"But…but…."

"I haven't got time to argue with you Maddie,

Jax's life is at stake!"

"... And yours?"

Jake tried hard to ignore her, the way he did when his mother was pestering him to clean his room or finish a chore. He had to stay focused if he and Jax had any hope of staying alive. Back in the arena, the bull paused for a moment, stomping its front hooves on the ground, grunting, and growling to itself. Prepared with a weapon, the hiatus gave Jake time to enter the stage before the animal felt inclined to charge again. Whilst on the floor, Jax lay stunned from the fall. He groaned with pain, every bone in his body felt bruised and battered. He tried with all his might to get up but each time he did, he faltered and collapsed again. Sensing Jax's vulnerability, the animal began to run at him. But before it gained momentum Jake came up behind and hit it forcefully with the cactus plant on its hind quarter. The animal cried with pain and turned around to face Jake. It was very angry and charged at Jake who managed to move out of the way and hit it again as it sped past. The bull stumbled; the deadly poison in the plant's prickles was beginning to take effect. The beast seemed to have the strength of a small army and chased Jake again and again until he found himself cornered with no escape. Jake felt the bull's horn pierce his skin and then he was thrown into the air and everything from that moment seemed to go in slow motion. He thought of his parents, home, and of Maddie as his body cascaded down to the ground until everything went black, as though in a long, peaceful sleep.

"Jake!" Screamed Maddie from the wings. The prince had to stop Maddie from running into the arena.

"Jake!" She screamed again, "Let me go!"

"It's too dangerous Maddie! But look!"

He was pointing at Jax, who by this time was back on his feet and ready to fight. He and the animal were face to face, both breathing heavily. Their eyes met and, in an instant, it became clear, that neither Jax nor the unfortunate beast wanted to be there fighting but were simply casualties in the chaos of Draxa's ungodly reign.

Jax thought of the prince, who was like a brother to him, and the bull imagined grazing in a lush, green field, just as the poison overwhelmed its mighty form and it dropped down dead onto the ground. Through complete shock, Jax didn't breathe for a full thirty seconds and then fought for some air to his lungs, his body shaking and trembling in the aftermath. The crowd cheered and applauded the victory, for it didn't happen often, but the only thing Jax could see was Jake's lifeless body on the floor. Before he could get to him both Maddie and the Prince were at his side.

"Jake! Jake! Are you alright? Wake up! Please!!!!" Maddie cried, distraught, "Is he dead? Oh, please don't be dead! JAKE!"

The prince felt for a pulse; it was weak and hard to find but eventually, after an excruciating pause, he found it.

"No. He's not dead but he will be soon if we don't get this wound attended to. We have to find a doctor immediately."

Jake moved his head and groaned, and the

audience cheered for him, but the Master of Ceremonies was a feared.

"You need to leave immediately! When the Queen finds out about your victory she will be incensed."

"A Doctor?"

"Take him back to my chamber. I will send a doctor to you and then you must go, and don't ever come back here. Do you understand?"

Maddie, the Prince and Jax nodded in unison and gently lifted Jake between them. The Master of Ceremonies watched them as they left the arena and said to himself,

..........*and there goes my knighthood. Ah well.*

CHAPTER SEVENTEEN

Out At Sea

Jake and Jax recovered quickly from their ordeal. Jake's injury proved to be less life threatening than at first thought, and the doctor stitched him up without much ado. Maddie practically pounced on him the minute he was released from the doctor's care. Fortunately, the elation he felt from being alive far outweighed any remnants of pain and her jumping and squealing, like an excited puppy, filled him with a great sense of relief and happiness.

"Steady, steady Mads," he said gently.

"Oh Jake! Jake! I thought you were dead!"

She hugged him so tight he thought she would never let go.

"Don't ever do that to me again Jake Applegate!"

"I'll try not to, ok?"

The two friends smiled at each other.

"Okay," said the prince, "if everyone is ready, we need to be on our way towards Tora South. Pitvas is going to meet us there with his brother, Weyo. I don't want to miss them."

"Yes, your Majesty," they replied in unison.

They got their bearings southward and carried on with their quest to reunite the magic quill with the magic scroll. They carried on their journey walking by the coast, from the Arena, to the south-easterly shore and hoped to find Keirs at the southernmost tip of the island. They walked, albeit slowly, the rest of the day and only rested as the sun began to yearn for its bed and the stars and the moon took its place in a festival of light. They made a small camp and bedded down for the duration. In the morning, they carried on their quest, the near-death experience at the arena making them eager to complete the task at hand and get back to a normal life, both here and back in America. With not too much distance now between them and Tora South they decided there would be no harm in taking a well-earned break. It was, as always, a very hot day and the pull of the cool ocean was hard to resist. The four pared down to under garments, kicked off their shoes, and squealed and laughed as they dove into the frothy waves. For a moment they felt like the children they were, without a care in the world.

"This is the life!" Said Jake beaming, and truly he was glad to still have one.

"Oh yes!" Replied Maddie, who in turn splashed the prince in a flurry of salt water

"Your Majesty! Look!" Exclaimed Jax, pointing in front of him.

To everyone's delight there appeared right in front of them a pod of dolphins, their mouths open, almost as if they were smiling and they made a clicking, squeaking noise.

"I've never seen them so close!" Said Maddie, "Have you Jake?"

"No never!"

Suddenly, one of the dolphins swam between Jake's legs and heaved him onto his back.

"Whoa!" He yelled.

Before they knew what was happening, they were all astride a dolphin.

"Looks like we are going for a ride! Hang on tight everyone!"

The children held on for their lives as the pod of dolphins dove and jumped out of the water, like horses on a merry-go-round. Maddie clenched tight with her thighs the way she had been taught at her local stables; however, this was much trickier without a saddle. Every now and then, each dolphin seemed to peer back at its rider, almost as if to reassure, and with a silent understanding of how welcome this distraction was. The spray of the water was exhilarating, and the children laughed and laughed. After a while, the pod came to a full stop and bobbed up and down in the water. They were facing away from land and out towards the horizon and just on the precipice there appeared a ship.

"Look!" Exclaimed Jake

"Isn't that the same ship we saw when we first left Tora Jake?"

"Looks like it."

"There's no mistaking it," offered the prince, "that is Deyjam's slave ship."

"Those poor little children!" Added Maddie.

"We need to get back to shore your Highness," urged Jax.

"You're right. There is nothing we can do to help them now. We will rescue them when we have taken back the throne from Draxa. I promise."

The children all looked at each other, a silent agreement that did not sit well but was, it seemed, the right course of action at this moment in time. Suddenly, the dolphins took off in the direction of the slave ship. There was nothing the children could do but hold on tight or risk being dumped in the middle of the ocean without any hope of being able to swim such a long distance to shore. They all knew to keep deathly quiet as they approached the ship. They stopped at the bow which boasted an elaborate fixture a bit like a wooden tower or tree house. There was a balcony which, at this moment in time, was empty, and above it another small storey from which a woman's sad face peered out. They heard a scurry of little feet running along the ship's deck and in a few moments a group of tear-stained children appeared over the balcony's edge.

"Are you here to take us home?" A little boy with angelic, curly hair asked.

The rest of the group jumped up and down excitedly with misplaced anticipation. A lump came to Maddie's throat at the sight of the little souls desperate to be back with their families.

"Shush now my darlings," the face of the woman in the second storey said soothingly, "you have to keep quiet so as not to disturb Deyjam."

"Yes Nanny," they all said quietly.

"Nanny?" The prince recoiled in horror.

"Yes, your Majesty, for I do recognise you

and I can see from your reaction that you recognise me also. I was indeed your sweet mother's nanny and then maid to Draxa, or should I say witch, for it is true, she is the old hag, Hec, mysteriously risen from her grave."

"So, it is true?" Exclaimed Jake, "Pitvas was right."

"When I found out her secret, she split me in two, my good self-entombed in the timbers of this ship and my bad self, back at Tora, North to do Hec's bidding."

"This confirmation," said the prince, "makes it all the more urgent for us to reunite the magic quill to the scroll and take our kingdom back from the clutches of that evil harpie."

"I wish you luck, your Highness, for I fear as long as Draxa is in power I will never escape this prison, or these little babes either."

Suddenly, the medallion around Maddie's neck began to vibrate,

"Guys its Bubo! Bubo! Bubo! Are you there?"

It took a second for the medallion to reveal the identity of the caller.

"No deary, it's not Master Bubo. He is somewhat incapacitated at the moment. He seems to be having a spot of bother with some wretched chains and a pot of hot oil ready for his roasting."

"Oh no!" Maddie recoiled in horror, "please, please... don't hurt him."

"Well, that would depend on you my dear. I take it you have my scroll?"

Maddie looked at the prince for guidance who then put his index finger to his lip and shook his head to quiet her. He beckoned for her to give him the medallion. He looked into it and saw, once again, the architect of the kingdom's misery.

"Well, well, well," said the Queen, "I should have known you'd have a hand in this treachery Prince Michaon. I would send your brother's regards, but the babbling fool has no idea who you are!"

The queen let out a spine-chilling cackle.

"It is your treachery that has brought misery to Tora Island, and I will make you pay!"

"Fighting words Prince Michaon and believe me, I relish the challenge, but if you don't bring the scroll back to me, it will be too late for your accomplice, Master Bubo."

With that threat, her vile image disappeared from sight and the children all looked at each other dazed.

"Without Bubo," said Jake fearfully, "we won't be able to get back home."

The thought that they could be stuck here forever left Maddie and Jake shaken.

"It would be as though we had never left. That's what he promised, didn't he Maddie?"

Silence reigned momentarily until they were woken from their stupor by the stomping of great feet, the reverberation of which could be felt even as they bobbed in the water, on the backs of the dolphins.

"What is going on here?!" Deyjam bellowed.

"Quick, you must leave, before he sees you," warned Good Nanny.

Before they knew what was happening, the ogre's mighty form appeared before them, and he scrambled at them like a cat catching mice. The little babes screamed and cried with fear, and in a split second, which seemed an eternity and played out almost as if in slow motion, Maddie was caught.

"Let go of me! Let go of me!" She screamed.

"The more you wriggle the tighter my grasp, young missy."

The ogre gave an almighty sniff with his big red nose, as though trying to absorb her whole being, and said with glee,

"I can always smell the unwanted scent of a troublesome stranger to our shores!"

"Maddie! Maddie!" Jake shouted helplessly.

"Finish the quest, Jake. It's our only hope... mine and Bubo's."

With that, she had the foresight to throw the magic scroll, which had been strapped over her shoulder in its leather container, into the air and into the hands of her best friend.

"Keep it safe! I know you will come back for me!"

"No Maddie! I won't leave you!"

"She's right Jake! We must leave… now!"

In his heart, Jake understood finishing the quest was key to saving Maddie, Bubo, and the other prisoners on the slave ship. However, as they locked eyes, he couldn't help but feel he was abandoning his best friend and who's to say when they would see each other again, if ever?

Then, with an even greater sense of urgency, the boys nudged the dolphins with their thighs and sped off towards the shore.

CHAPTER EIGHTEEN

KIERS

Back on the beach, Jake dropped to his knees at the sight of Maddie's abandoned shoes.

"Take them," said Jax gently, "she'll need them when we rescue her."

Jake nodded his head and they prepared themselves for their journey southward.

Without Maddie to energise the scroll, we must navigate ourselves. We were walking this way before, so I think it's best to continue. Once the dark falls, if we look for the North Star, we will be able to get our bearings," said the prince confidently.

"Agreed," said Jake and Jax.

The prince led the way, with Jake in the middle and Jax bringing up the rear. All were consumed in their own thoughts, and each gave a quick, backward glance at Deyjam's slave ship and hoped that Maddie would be okay.

They had been travelling for a few hours without respite, when Jax suggested,

"I think we should spear some fish for dinner before it gets too dark; we'll need all our wits and strength to out man the ogre, Keirs."

"Good idea," agreed the prince.

"I can't think of anything except for Maddie," said Jake forlornly.

"The best thing you can do for Maddie, Jake, is to stay strong for her. Now, let's get dinner," Prince Michaon said firmly.

Jake knew he was right, and the boys withdrew their swords and went, waist deep, into the sea. The trio, including Jake, were all now proficient hunters and made an ideal team. In the setting sun, they moved stealthily, each knowing what the other was trying to communicate without saying a word. Jax was out in front, ever the intrepid scout, his dark hair and silhouette almost camouflaged in the dying light. Jake and the Prince, on the other hand, shone bright like beacons, thanks to identical mops of blonde hair. It was uncanny how alike they were; they even moved in the same way. All three, still just boys, but with the fate of Whole Island, laid firmly at their feet.

Fish caught and cooking on a campfire; the boys sat around and stared into the hypnotic flames. After a short time of silent reflection, Jax looked up into the night sky and pointed saying,

"Your Majesty, the North Star, is it not?"

"Yes, came the reply, and from its position, we can see that we are on the right track. Eat up comrades and bunk down, for tomorrow there will be a reckoning on Tora Island."

Jax and Jake did as they were bid and settled to sleep on makeshift beds of grass and leaves. As slumber came upon them, their eyes were drawn to the light of the North Star, its light was comforting and seemed to watch over them like an absent mother.

Meanwhile, two other dispirit figures gazed upon the bright star, one was Maddie, the other Queen Draxa, otherwise known as the old witch, Hec. Both were transfixed in quiet contemplation, one on the side of good, the other on the side of evil, each hoping their cause would prevail.

After a good night's rest, the boys set off at first light. They walked for quite some time without any proper rest, only stopping to take a quick swig of water, for they were each spurred on by the lives dependent on the quest's success: Maddie, Bubo, the enslaved children, and the whole population of Tora Island. They had no idea how far they had walked until, collapsing on the ground with exhaustion, they looked up to see, in the distance, land's end and the sparsely inhabited homestead of Tora, South. The boys each gulped with a sense of fear and trepidation, but luckily for them, the single occupant of this region, the ogre, Kiers, had yet to be seen.

"Look at the fields and pastures filled with bulls, cows and their young," said Jax, pointing over yonder, "this is what was in his eyes, that awful day at the arena."

"Who Jax?" Asked, the prince.

"The bull, or the beast SHE turned him into. He just wanted to be here, with his family, the same as everyone else."

The boys suddenly felt very weary and lonesome for their own kith and kin.

"We did what we had to do Jax," replied the prince, "and when we take back the kingdom, the bull, wherever he is, will be grateful that no more of his kind will have to fight, ever again."

Jake put his arm around his shoulder, to comfort him, and they began to walk towards the herd of cattle. Suddenly, their senses were confused by what they thought was a loud growl of thunder, even though the day shone bright and dry. The thunderous roar turned into garbled sounds and then a venomous command,

"Stay away from my babies! You will die for what you have done! You killed him! You killed him! You killed my son!"

The mighty ogre, Keirs was hurtling towards them and in their defence the prince shouted,

"We had no choice!"

"Yes! You had a choice, you could have died instead and now, by the gods, you will!"

Keirs was by far the largest and most fierce ogre the children had encountered, as yet. His mighty form, clad only in shorts, knee length Grecian style sandals and two gold bands around his arms, was a formidable sight.

"Swords at the ready!" Prince Michaon ordered.

Jake and Jax did as they were bid, and their weapons glinted proudly in the sunlight. Keirs had nothing but his huge hands, which were both curled into a tight fist, ready for battle. His large, lumbering body was slow and clumsy and each time he tried to hit the children, they were able to move quickly out of the way, the blow pummelling the ground and sending a plume of debris into the air.

"Keep still you vermin! When I catch you, I

will rip your insides out!"

"I'd like to see you try, slow poke!" Said Jake feeling more confident at the ogre's lack of speed.

"Why you.........!"

Keirs chased Jake around the field, the earth quaking each time his massive foot hit the ground. Jake faced the ogre, walking backwards and baiting him with every step. Suddenly, he lost his footing on an uneven lump of turf and toppled over into a heap. The ogre saw his chance and grabbed Jake by the leg and pulled him towards him. His vice like grip clamped hold of him like a boa constrictor hugging its prey.

"I am going to squash you like the bug you are!" He declared and lifted Jake above his head, ready to send him hurtling to his death.

"Help! Help!" Cried Jake, unable to prize himself free.

Instinctively, Prince Michaon and Jax launched themselves onto Kiers bare back, piercing his body with their blades. However, given the ogre's sheer mass, their attempts proved to be no more consequential than a mere gnat bite, and their predicament only served to make him laugh, with even more relish.

"You foolish little creatures!" Said Kiers, and with his free hand he scooped the Prince and Jax off his back and dangled them by their tabards right in front of his face. Jake was in his other hand, and they looked at each other, trying desperately to think of a way out of their predicament. The ogres face loomed large, each pore in his skin like a chasm, each breath hitting them like a toxic gale.

In the distance, the sound of singing could be heard and Keirs immediately turned his head as though he recognised the tune.

"What on earth?" He said confused, the children still wriggling in grasp.

Walking towards them was the ogre, Pitvas with his skittishes and, as he had promised, by his side was his brother, Weyo. The youngest ogre was massive, towering a good head and shoulders above his brother, Kiers. Again, he was clad in only shorts, Grecian style sandals and sporting a gold band on each arm. He had a happy, smiling face and sang continuously as he and Pitvas walked towards them.

"Well, look... what... we... have... here," said Kiers, in a low, bloodthirsty voice, each word spat out in sheer, simmering rage.

"Steady now Keirs," replied Pitvas, in a big brother sort of way, "you and our brother, Deyjam, are under the spell of the evil witch, Hec, risen from her grave."

"Liar! The witches are all dead!"

"Yes, they are. All but one. Hec is alive! Now put the children down, you don't really want to hurt them, do you?"

Keirs let out a huge growl before throwing the children to the ground and then lunged at his brothers. Pitvas' strength was his wisdom, so he decided to leave the fighting to Weyo, who simply held Keirs abreast with just one hand, leaving the disgruntled ogre thrashing and kicking to no avail. Once Kiers had worn himself out, Weyo twirled him around and quickly tied his hands and feet with rope and secured it with a handcuff knot.

"I knew that rope would come in handy," said Pitvas congratulating himself.

"Pitvas! Pitvas! Thank goodness you came when you did, otherwise we would have been toast!"

"Ah! Boys! Your Majesty," He said bowing respectfully at Prince Michaon, "at your service. Allow me to introduce my youngest brother, Weyo."

"Pleasure to meet you, Weyo," said the boys in unison.

"I'm afraid you won't get a sensible reply from him as he is bewitched by Hec, as all my brothers are. He will only sing and smile for the time being, until we can break the spell."

"Even so," said the prince, "we are indebted to you both."

"Pitvas! Deyjam has Maddie! We have to rescue her!" Pleaded Jake.

"Deyjam... Maddie... what happened?"

".........and Draxa, I mean Hec, has Bubo. She knows everything!" Added Jax.

"Quickly then, your Majesty, time is of the essence, we must find the quill and rescue Maddie before it is too late!"

"But where do we start?" questioned Jake.

"I'll never tell you!" Growled Kiers.

"If I know my brother, it will be in his shelter. I am sure it won't be hard to find, he is all brawn and no brains! Let's go."

They spread out and searched as much ground as they could until they came across a massive entrance to a cavern, built into the mountainous terrain of the island.

"This is it," said Pitvas with great certainty, "Weyo and I will go first."

Inside, the cavern was lit with torches attached to the walls. Their flames emitted a homely glow, and the children were surprised at how inviting the shelter appeared. There was a very large bed in one corner, which was made from logs and sported a couple of fine blankets. A fireplace had been dug out and a chimney was fashioned with island stone, releasing its smoke up and out of the mound of earth. On the grate was a big pot of vegetable stew and a large, wooden rocking chair took centre stage in front of the hearth. Next to it, was a table, which was overflowing with drawings of the ogres' precious cattle and on top of those was a solitary jar, containing pencils and chalks.

"It couldn't possibly be that simple," said the prince, pointing at the jar.

"What couldn't be?" Asked Jake.

"That!" Said Jax, again, pointing at the Jar.

"Jumping Jehoshaphat!" Exclaimed Jake, "It's the magic quill!"

"Just as I thought," said Pitvas, picking it up, "all brawn and no brains."

"How do we know it is the real thing?" Asked Jake.

"We don't," replied Prince Michaon, "not without Maddie to finish the portrait. But as there is nothing else here and the feather looks a match with Bubo's, I would hazard a guess it is."

The group made their way back to Kiers where Pitvas instructed his trusty skittish, Oreo to watch over him.

"Give him plenty of food and water Oreo. He's not a bad lad really! We'll come back for him when we've taken back the kingdom!"

They all cheered, for this was the first time, in a long time, that they felt hopeful for their quest's success.

CHAPTER NINETEEN

DEYJAM

Deyjam's slave ship bobbed rhythmically atop a calm sea, keeping the children quiet and sending them to sleep. The ship was anchored and moored to a small jutting of land in the island's peninsula water, which was surrounded by the cities of Tora North, Tora Northwest, Tora Mid-West, Tora South, Arena City and Tora Northeast. The land served as a walkabout for the ogre, Deyjam, to stretch his legs and occasionally, he would let the children disembark and run around the grassy mount.

Maddie sat crossed legged on the deck below good Nanny's balcony. She felt so sorry for the kind lady trapped in the ship's timbers that she felt compelled to stay with her, to keep her company and her spirits up. The rag taggle of Tora's children sent to the slave ship grew larger every day and they lay all around Maddie, inching closer and closer for comfort and nestling in her lap. They were very frightened and so Maddie gently soothed their brows, whilst humming a lullaby her mother used to sing.

"You are a natural, my dear. Do you have brothers and sisters?" Asked Good Nanny.

"No, just me, and my mom and dad. Mom says I am more than enough trouble for her to handle. I guess Jake is the closest thing I have to a brother......"

Maddie couldn't help the tears from running down her cheeks.

"Don't cry, my dear. Goodness will prevail and Queen Draxa will be defeated. Prince Michaon and his brother, Prince Ladon, are cut from the same cloth as the old king, courageous, fierce, and stubbornly loyal."

"I don't doubt that Nanny, but where are they? It's been days now. What if they haven't found the magic quill? What if the ogre Kiers has captured them? It doesn't matter what cloth you are cut from if you are in chains!"

"Hush now child, you will wake the others. Now look at me Maddie."

Maddie did as she was bid.

"I can see by just looking at you that you are strong willed. I wonder that you have ever given up on anything. Rather, you are like a dog with a bone, tenacious and persistent, am I right?"

Maddie nodded her head.

"Did your mentor, Master Bubo give you any advice?"

"Yes, he told me to count to ten and then think before I acted."

"Sound advice, Maddie. Think your situation through, don't react to it. Your fear is getting the better of you. You must think practically and with a rational head, my dear."

"Yes, Nanny, you're right. I have to get hold of myself."

They could hear the large, lumbering footsteps of the ogre, Deyjam, as he returned from his daily walk about. He came straight to the deck where Maddie was sitting with the children.

He was very large, but not as large as Kiers and nowhere near as big as the loveable, Weyo. He wore a grey, belted tunic and had a thick mop of grey hair to match. However, it was his huge, long nose, which stood at a perfect right angle to his face that took centre stage. It shone as bright as a Belisha beacon, but the same colour as a shiny, red apple. It constantly twitched, picking up scents of threat or prey. He could even pick up the scent of Maddie's salty tears,

"Been crying again, little baby, boo hoo," he said mimicking her and pretending to rub his eyes. He may not have been the strongest of the ogres, but he was the meanest.

"Leave her alone Deyjam!" Ordered Good Nanny

"Oh, shut up old woman or I will sew up

your meddling mouth!"

Deyjam seemed particularly agitated today and Nanny did as she was told.

"Something smells amiss," he said to himself, and he took in three deep breaths but could not detect anything untoward.

"No matter, as soon as the ship is filled to the brim with children, we will be sailing to meet your new masters." He laughed a loud, heartless laugh and the children, now awake, clung even closer to Maddie.

Peculiarly, the water at the bow of the ship became rough and choppy, even though the sea was calm.

"That's strange," said Deyjam, and he walked over to the bow and leaned over.

The sea below him was churning like a cyclone and before he knew what was happening, Weyo, with his brother Pitvas on his back, sprung from its depth like the God, Poseidon, erupting from his watery lair. The frothy spray, from Weyo's arms, looked like huge angel wings, its droplets landing on Maddie and the children.

"Thank goodness!" She said to herself, "we are saved!"

"I should have known!" Growled Deyjam, "I could smell my traitorous brothers a mile off!"

By this time Weyo and Pitvas were onboard and not far behind them were the Prince, Jake and Jax pulling up, starboard side, in a small rowing boat.

"Now Deyjam," said Pitvas, "you know we would never betray you. We are blood; we are one. You have been enchanted by Queen Draxa who is really the old witch, Hec, risen from her grave."

"Liar!" Shouted Deyjam, who then launched himself at Pitvas with such ferocity they both toppled backward, Deyjam landing on top of his brother. He began to strangle Pitvas with his massive hands, causing his face to turn a frightening shade of purple when, in the nick of time, Weyo, still smiling and singing, lifted him off so effortlessly, he may as well have been picking up a feather.

"There, Weyo, there," instructed Pitvas breathlessly, pointing to a pile of rope on the deck,

"Tie him up with that. Don't worry Deyjam, you will be freed when the spell is broken."

"I will get you! I will sell you all to the highest bidder!" Growled Deyjam.

"... and gag him brother. We don't need his racket giving our game away when we reach Tora North."

In the meantime, Jake and the Prince ran to Maddie, quickly untying her. Jake hugged her so tightly she thought he was going to crush her ribs.

"I knew you'd come!" She cried.

"Maddie, I... was... so... worried," Jake's emotions were so heightened, he could hardly speak.

"I am so glad you are safe Maddie," said the prince, "however, the time for reunion must wait, for we must make haste."

"Of course," replied Maddie, still enveloped in Jake's hug, "I understand."

"We must make sail to Tora North. The time to take our kingdom back is now."

He turned to look at the huddle of children, their eyes opened wide with fright and said,

"You will be back with your families before the day is out…"

The children at first were bemused and then when the reality of his words took hold, they ran to him, embracing him so hard he nearly lost his balance.

"Steady now steady," he instructed the children, "but you must promise me one thing?"

They all nodded their heads eagerly to their savoir.

"You must all promise to stay as quiet as a mouse when we reach Tora North. Our lives depend on it."

They all nodded their heads in unison and sat back down on the deck obediently.

"Your Majesty... your Majesty," Prince Michaon heard a familiar voice, one that eased his poor heart.

"Up here, your Majesty, above your head."

"Nanny! Oh Nanny! I hate seeing you imprisoned like this!"

"Please don't fret your Highness, it's not as bad as it looks, and I know you will release me when the evil Hec is dead. I just wanted to see your sweet face once more."

Their eyes locked momentarily, and in that moment, Prince Michaon felt the pain of loss so deeply he could hardly breathe. He missed his father and mother, but most of all he missed his big brother and the carefree life that once belonged to them. They were so close to victory, he could feel it in his very core, and he was more determined than ever to succeed.

"Listen up everyone..." ordered the prince, and the group gathered around him.

"This is the most dangerous part of our journey. It is time to face Hec head on and there is no knowing if we will triumph or die trying?"

He looked at each person in his small band of brothers and said,

"The task to free Tora Island from the grip of evil is ours and, as the true King's representative, I wish you luck and thank you from the bottom of my heart."

Maddie and Jake looked at each other and Jake gave Maddie a wink and squeezed her hand. She was scared, there was no doubting it.

"But first, there is one more thing we have to do before we set sail. Jax, will you do the honours?"

Jax took out the magic scroll from its container and also, the magic quill, which had been placed with it for safe keeping. They both started to energise a luminous green gold colour as it came closer to Maddie. She held them in her shaking hands and Jake said softly,

"You know what you have to do, Mads."

Nodding her head she said quietly, "yes."

CHAPTER TWENTY

The Final Battle... Weyo!

Bubo had been a prisoner in the castle tower for some days now. His cell mate was the royal amnesiac, Prince Ladon who, like himself, was chained at the wrist. The prince showed no signs of remembering who he was and appeared mentally vacant to those who saw him. Bubo hoped, beyond hope, that the children were safe and their quest for the magic quill had been successful, but in his heart, he did not hold out much hope and feared that Tora Island was beyond saving. He sunk his head into his feathery chest despairingly and prayed for a miracle and then, as though by some good magic, Prince Ladon, seemed to rouse from his stupor.

"Prince Ladon?.........Your Majesty?..........."

He said nothing and blinked his eyes repeatedly.

"Do you recognise me? Do you know where you are?"

The prince didn't reply, and Bubo's heart sank once again.

"Master Bubo? Is that you? What is the meaning of this and why am I in chains?" He shook his bonds forcibly, but they would not relinquish their hold.

"Thank the gods, thank the gods! Your Highness, you must listen to me very carefully."

"Unchain me Bubo this instant, I command you!"

"Please Sire, for your sake, mine, and Tora Island, you must be quiet," whispered Bubo.

"Queen Draxa cannot know that you have recovered your memory, just yet, for she is the architect of our misery. Her power is a dark magic which trumps mine hands down."

"But why can't I remember any of this and where is my brother?"

"The Queen used magic to take your memories and your throne, Sire. Your brother, Prince Michaon, escaped her clutches and has been on a quest, to unite the magic scroll with the magic quill and break the spell that bound you. And thank the gods, the quest has been successful for you have come back to us!"

"But if the Queen's magic is so powerful, how will we defeat her Bubo?"

"She used one of my feathers to make the quill and it zapped my powers, but once I have it back, my powers will return strong enough to challenge hers, your Majesty. Also, we have the brute strength of the mighty ogre, Pitvas on our side. He is with Prince Michaon and his allies. If we can rally the people, we might be able to overpower the Queen and her henchmen. But first, we must escape and try to find your brother, for I am sure he is on his way. We have to get the keys from the guard. When I get his attention, you overpower him."

The prince nodded in agreement and Bubo moaned loudly, clutching his tummy.

"Guard! Guard! I need help!"

"What is it now, you old crow?" The Queen's guard asked irritably, looking through the bars of the cell door.

"I am ill," feigned Bubo, "I need to see a doctor urgently!"

The guard had been on duty for a good twelve hours, without respite, and Bubo prayed his weariness would be his undoing. He unlocked the cell door huffing and puffing as he did so.

"Yes... well?" He asked Bubo impatiently, "what's the matter with you?"

Bubo pointed towards his tummy.

"Here...come closer and you will see. I hope you're not squeamish?"

The guard leaned in, grumbling to himself. Just as he bent over, Prince Ladon came up behind him and wrapped his chains around his neck.

"Just so he passes out your Majesty, advised Bubo, "there has been enough death in this kingdom to last a lifetime."

The guard struggled but Prince Ladon was a strong young man, with the reclamation of his throne as impetus. The guard lost consciousness and slipped to the floor.

"His keys your Majesty!" Bubo pointed to a bunch of skeleton keys hanging from the guard's belt.

"Quickly, unlock our chains and then restrain him. We must escape the walls of the castle before Draxa suspects anything and find Prince Michaon. Oh, and one last thing Prince Ladon."

"Yes, Bubo? What is it?"

"May the gods protect us, for this final battle will change everything, for better or for worse."

Before the slave ship set sail for Tora North, Jax had the good sense to send an obliging seagull messenger to his mother Esmeralda, the castle cook, to let her know of their plans and to rally the people, without suspicion. The bird landed on the side of the ship and stared directly at Jax. He knew the bird was here to help and hoped that it was a good omen for them.

They made good time and dropped anchor, not directly in front of the castle or, more importantly, in front of Draxa's balcony where she habitually stood to survey her conquest, but adjacent to it, where the people waited, and the children could quietly disembark.

It brought a tear to the eye of anyone witnessing the reunion between parent and child and one could not help but be moved by the tightest of embrace, which vanquished the fears of perpetual separation.

From the port side of the ship the Prince, Maddie, Jake, Jax, Pitvas and Weyo watched as the population of Tora North gathered near the harbour. They recognised Prince Michaon, of that there was no doubt, and they waited for their ruler to command them. Prince Michaon was moved by their allegiance and, for a moment, was lost in thought.

"People of Tora North and our other cities.

The throne has been usurped by a vile infiltrator. Queen Draxa is really the old witch Hec, risen from her ungodly grave. She has sought to destroy my family and to oppress yours! We must attack the castle fortress before we lose the advantage of surprise. Who is with me?!!"

There was a worrying hush amongst the crowd, their fear evident. Suddenly, there was a great gust of wind overhead and flying towards them was Bubo, his large wingspan heralding a new beginning for Tora Island.

"Bubo! It's Bubo!" Cried Maddie, the sight of him made her yearn for home and he landed on the rim of the ship, next to her and the other children.

"I am with you!" A solitary voice called out, but it was not Bubo's and came from the back of the gathering.

Silence reigned, and slowly, slowly the people parted, bowing low and with reverence.

"Ladon! Oh Ladon! My brother!" Prince Michaon exclaimed, running towards him and hugging him tightly.

Maddie and Jake glanced at each other, as did Pitvas and Weyo, each trying to contain their emotions, for it was a sight to behold.

"Brother," said Michaon, "I thought I'd lost you forever!"

"… And it is you and your dear friends I have to thank for my return and not a minute too late. We have the most important battle of our lives to fight!"

The population of Tora Island let out a loud cheer and even in such a small space of time, word was spreading, and more and more subjects were arriving to lend their support. They had had enough, and the time was now to take back their country.

"Everyone!" Announced Prince Ladon, "Arm yourselves and make ready to fight for our kingdom, or die trying, lest we remain slaves to our ruthless oppressor!"

The young children who narrowly escaped their internment on the slave ship were taken to a safe place before the battle commenced. Once that was done, everyone and anyone who could carry a weapon did so. The princes, Bubo, Jake, Jax, Maddie and the two ogres led the way to the castle and the sheer might of the crowd rammed at the gates until they bowed and broke free. The guards on duty were taken by surprise, overwhelmed by the crowd, and left incapacitated and dazed. The angry throng ran through the courtyard and into the great, main hall, where Draxa was sitting on her throne waiting for them. She sat resplendent in her jewel encrusted gown, arranged just so for maximum impact. It was just a shame her cold heart did not match its beauty.

"So, it has come to this?" Princes Ladon and Michaon, "lovely to see you in such fine fettle."

She got up and walked towards the children, Bubo, and the ogres, circling each one in turn, poking at their faces with her long scrawny finger.

"Master Bubo, I can tell that you have your precious feather back and Ladon his memory, but do you really think you are powerful enough to challenge me?"

Still enveloping the band of friends, she

moved slowly and with calculated precision, like a tiger stalking its prey.

"Pitvas, I see you have escaped your leafy tomb, but your brother is still a singing fool," and she let out a spine-chilling laugh.

"... and finally, who do we have here?"

She stared directly at Maddie and Jake, holding their gaze for an uncomfortable length of time. Maddie thought she was going to throw up and Jake hoped to himself that the trembling in his legs was not obvious.

"The game is over Hec, for we all know who you really are," declared Prince Ladon, "and I will have my throne back!"

The crowd cheered and raised their weapons in the air.

"Is that so?" answered Hec, "I suppose I won't be needing this anymore," whipping the mask from her face to reveal her wizened and craggy face.

A communal gasp of horror reverberated around the great hall.

"Battle if we must, subjects of Tora Island," announced the old witch, "but know this, you will lose, and I will make your lives worse for your impudence."

There was an audible mumble amongst the crowd and each citizen turned to their neighbour for courage.

"But before we start, I have a little surprise for you, boy."

The old witch, Hec, pointed her long, taloned finger at Jake and then ordered,

"Nanny! Bring out the prisoner!"

The children looked at each other confused. They could not imagine what evil deed could excite the old crone so. Suddenly, into the main hall, bad Nanny, with a triumphant grimace on her face, brought in an old woman, handcuffed, and shackled in chains.

"Grandma? She has my grandma!" Cried Jake.

"Jakie? Jakie? Is that you? What's happening? Am I dreaming?"

Mrs Applegate answered in return.

"Your medallion, Master Bubo, has relinquished many secrets, including the inhabitants of 200 Scott Drive!"

She now spoke directly to the nucleus of the rebellion, namely the princes, Jake, Maddie, Jax and the ogres.

"Surrender yourselves and the old woman and the people of Tora will be spared."

"Never!" Cried Prince Ladon and he led the people in a battle cry, thrashing his sword into the air.

The newly initiated army thrust forward, fighting hand to hand with Hec's guards. The witch flung Mrs. Applegate to the floor, rendering her unconscious. Maddie rushed over to her, taking her by the arm, and dragged her to a safe alcove. She, thankfully, found a pulse and prayed the impact sustained by the old woman was not life threatening. Turning around, she witnessed the great hall transformed into a battle ground, with the princes, Jake, Jax and the ogres in the thick of it. The citizens of Tora outnumbered the witch's guards and it seemed, for a moment, they had the upper hand. However, her heart sank when she realised Hec was conjuring a spell and a moment later, all of the statues and portraits in the room came alive to aid the old witch. A number of Tora's citizens had already succumbed to the expertise of the guards and now the statues and portraits entered the fracas, without any apparent weakness, the citizens dropped like a domino train. Pitvas and Weyo struggled to keep their attackers off them, and they crawled over their bodies like an army of ants. Hec and Bubo were locked together, wing to hand, in a stalemate of magic energy. Its force shone an electric blue colour, and it was only a matter of time until one overpowered the other. The princes and Jax fought bravely, and it was only when Maddie saw Jake, with a blade against his throat the world fell away, and everything seemed to go in slow motion. Inside her head she screamed, and her instinct was to rush to him, but she stopped, for a split second, and remembered what Bubo had told her, "Think before you act Maddie." She quickly surveyed the room, hoping a solution would present itself. It was useless, she was useless; all she could focus on was Weyo, ironically, still singing as he staved off death or injury for as long as possible. Suddenly, the words he sang caught her attention:

"A young serving maid, dally dilly dally ho,
Worked hard through the day, with a heave and a ho,
She scrubbed with her water with a to and a fro,
Dally dilly, dally dilly, dally dilly, dally ho,
She stood at the top with the witch down below,
Over went her bucket, dally dilly, dally ho,
And drenched the old crone and a melting she did go,
Dally dilly, dally dilly, dally dilly, dally ho, ho, ho."

"He's singing about a witch! He's singing about a witch! I need water!" Maddie said to herself and remembered seeing a mop and bucket in the alcove where she hid Mrs. Applegate. She ran to it and sure enough the bucket was still filled with water. She grabbed it and ran towards Hec, throwing its contents over her. The old hag screamed,

"No! Not again! I'll have you!" She spewed her dying threat at Maddie and proceeded to melt to the ground like a candle end.

Instantly, the statues and portraits crashed to the floor and the guards dropped their swords, for their entrancement was also broken.

"What have you done? Mistress! Oh my Mistress!"

"She is not your mistress," good Nanny's softly spoken voice explained to her other half. Their reunion was made possible by the witch's death and, each half, drawn automatically to the other to restore nature's balance.

"Come to me," said Good Nanny, and she held out her hand to her other half. Bad Nanny looked at her momentarily, her eyes lost and confused, and once they touched, they merged together, as one. The crowd let out a loud cheer and everyone hugged for their quest was a success and Tora Island was free from the tyranny of the old witch, Hec.

"Maddie," asked Bubo, "How did you know the water would kill Hec?"

"It was Weyo's song, all this time he held the answer with his verses."

"Brother," said Weyo to Pitvas, "thank the gods, I can speak again. I sang that song over and over again, but no one took any notice, until Maddie. I am indebted to you, young lady."

"We all are," added Prince Michaon, "and to you Jake. We couldn't have done this without you."

"Today we shall mourn our fallen," announced Prince Ladon, "but tomorrow, we will feast in honour of Maddie and Jake, strangers to our land, but kin in our hearts."

"After... will you take us home Bubo," asked Maddie.

"With pleasure," replied Bubo.

Suddenly there was a muffled cry and instinctively, everyone drew their swords.

"Oh goodness Jake! I forgot, it's your granny."

Allow me, offered Weyo, and he promptly lifted Mrs Applegate from the alcove, as though she were a feather, and held her in the crook of her arm. She looked around the room, at everyone in turn, gazing finally into the ogre's large eyes and said,

"This is the weirdest dream I have ever had. I must stop eating cheese before I go to bed!"

With that, all the friends started to giggle, which turned into belly laughs and then finally, tears of joy, for they were victorious.

CHAPTER TWENTY-ONE
Going Home

After the feast, Prince Ladon was crowned king of Tora Island with Prince Michaon standing by his side. The ogres went to free their brothers, Kiers and Deyjam, who, now free of their bewitchment, were so happy to be reunited as a family. They formed a massive huddle and hugged and hugged each other until they fell, exhausted and laughing onto the ground, its impact so strong the islanders thought there had been an earthquake. The bulls were freed to live out their lives in peace and harmony, without having to fight, and Kiers tended them like a doting father, with the help of Pitvas' skittishes, who gently nipped at their ankles like well trained, sheep dogs. Hec's sticky remains were taken to a secret hiding place and buried so deep in the ground nothing and no one would come across her, ever again. As for Maddie and Jake, once they had taken their leave from their Tora Island posse, giving each a long embrace goodbye, Bubo sat them on his wings, with grandma on his back, and traversed one universe to the other. As Bubo had said, they found themselves back where they started, same time, same place, as though nothing had ever happened.

"Goodbye Maddie and Jake of Connecticut, U.S.A. Tora Island salutes you!"

"Goodbye Bubo, we'll never forget you!" They said in unison as the large magic owl flew off into the distance. From that day on, Maddie checked herself before she acted impulsively, as was her nature to do, and Jake was never again scared of any bullies.

In the dim of the autumn, afternoon light, Mrs. Applegate woke from her cat nap, taken regularly in her favourite reclining chair, and wondered with a sigh.......... at her strange dream.

CPSIA information can be obtained
at www.ICGtesting.com
Printed in the USA
LVHW101936270522
719946LV00017B/700